Grand Teton Stampede

C. R. Fulton

THE CAMPGROUND KIDS
www.bakkenbooks.com

ISBN 978-1-955657-15-0
For Worldwide Distribution
Printed in the U.S.A.

PUBLISHED BY BAKKEN BOOKS
2022

To Isaiah and Raina,
I look forward to all the adventures ahead!

National Park Adventures: Series One
Grand Teton Stampede
Smoky Mountain Survival
Zion Gold Rush
Rocky Mountain Challenge
Grand Canyon Rescue

National Park Adventures: Series Two
Yellowstone Sabotage
Yosemite Fortune
Acadia Discovery
Glacier Vanishing
Arches Legend

For more books, check out:
www.bakkenbooks.com

- 1 -

I ease toward a dead log, knowing everything hinges on complete silence. Creeping through the forest on my hands and knees, shifting forward, I peer over the steep drop-off. The cougar will pass below me on the ridge any second...I just know it.

I'd heard its eerie scream, and since then I've been determined to see it. I hold my breath. *Was that a whisper of sound?*

Cocking my head, I focus hard, my nerves tingling. *He's close*—not on the narrow trail far below like I'd thought, but right here. I clutch the knife Poppa gave me, sliding open its blade.

Maybe I should have brought a bigger weapon...

It's a struggle to keep my breath from coming too loud in the stillness. If I could make it to the broad oak tree to my left, I could protect my back. There's another slim whisper of movement.

The longing to see him and the desire to run are at war in my mind. Nearby a crow caws; the sound jolts me into motion, and before I know it, the rough bark of the oak is gritting against my back. Searching wildly for the cougar, my foot tangles in a root. As I snatch at the tree, the knife slips from my grasp, and I suck in a harsh breath, goosebumps spreading.

He's behind the tree; he'll get my arm if I reach for the knife. Something grabs my shoulder, sending shock waves through my chest. I whirl away, thrashing at branches, shouting at the top of my lungs.

My little sister stands there with her hands on her hips. She's nine and as silent as an owl on the wing when she wants to be. "Isaiah, are you out here looking for a cougar?" she questions, with a look of disbelief.

I call her the queen of funny faces, and she's sure making one now.

"Yes, Sadie…until you showed up," I say, trying to sound normal, while my heart still slams into my ribs.

"Mr. Jenkins says there aren't any cougars in Kentucky, and there hasn't been for 50 years."

"Well, there's one now. I heard it scream."

Her eyes widen. "When?"

I look back down at the path, pick up the knife, knowing every chance of seeing him is ruined now. "When I took out the garbage for Grammy last week."

Grammy and Poppa live just down in a holler not a half a mile from our house. I wish we had land like them instead of living in a neighborhood with perfect little yards and only this tiny patch of woods to escape to.

She shrugs, the news making her eyes bright. "Mom told me to come and get you."

That message makes me grin. "Really?"

"Race you!" she says, then takes off through the woods.

"That's not fair!" I run after her, emerging from the small patch of woods, heading toward our house.

Even though I'm tall for a twelve-year-old, I'm big- boned like Dad, and I know I'll never beat her at a foot race when she has a head start. Still, I give it my best shot. Mom's calling us in early can only mean one thing: she and Dad have decided where we're heading for the last week of vacation before school starts.

"Please, oh, please," I pant, "not to Washington, D.C." All I've wanted to do this year is go camping. But sleeping in the backyard of our subdivision hasn't scratched that itch by a long shot. "Please not the city and dusty museums."

The thought of returning to school after vacation in less than two weeks sends a shiver of fear into my heart. Max Smith will be there, waiting for me. He hates my guts, and he never misses a chance to make fun of me.

I push away the awful thought and burst into the house. Mom is smiling widely. She loves museums. *Oh, no.* Sadie is jumping up and down, her hands over her mouth.

"Tell us!" she shouts through them.

I cringe; Dad's arms are folded across his chest. He's on my side, wanting an outdoor adventure. *This doesn't look good.* I clench my hands at my sides as Mom takes a deep breath to speak.

"Well..."

Sadie squeals. She'll be thrilled with whatever they've decided. *Come on, Mom.*

"Your dad and I have spent a lot of time on this decision. And I know there were many ideas for this vacation."

"Mom! Where are we going?" I can't keep the desperate tone out of my voice.

Her smile grows. "We are going to the Grand Teton National Park for a week of tent camping!"

A roar explodes from my mouth! My every dream has just come true! Sadie grabs me with her surprisingly strong bear hug. I can't help shouting again. "Yes!"

"All right, all right!" Dad is smiling now too. "We've got to gear up and make it to Wyoming in just three days."

"Wyoming! We're going to see bears, elk, moose, and pronghorn too! Aw, Mom!" I grab her around the waist, knowing she chose this destination just for me. "Thanks."

Arms around me, she looks down with an apprehensive expression. "Think I'm going to make it?"

"I'll make sure you do, Mom! I've read everything about camping, and you'll love it!"

Mom eyes Sadie and me. "The Grand Teton National Park is no joke though, okay? I need you both to use your smarts, pay attention to the rules, and most of all, stay safe."

"We will, Mom," we declare in unison.

"There's more," Dad says. "Your cousin Ethan is coming too, so you boys will have your own tent, and Sadie will stay with Mom and me."

"Aw." Sadie frowns at not having her own tent.

"What?! Ethan is coming?" I run around the room, leaping high and pumping my fist. Ethan is 14 and getting to spend a week in the wilds of Wyoming with him is more than I can handle. "Waaahooo!"

We load into Dad's truck and head for the sporting goods store. Mom hands Sadie and me a printout of our camping budget.

"Mom, what's a 'budge'?" Sadie asks.

"*Budget*, honey. It's the amount of money we're going to spend on this trip. See the red numbers at the top? Those are the things we can't change, like the gas to get there and back, the fees we must pay to get into the park and paying for the campsite and food. I want you both to list items that are most important for us to have while camping."

For the first time, knowing math makes sense to me. I write, my pen barely able to keep up with my mind.

☐ Waterproof tents

- ☐ Sleeping bags
- ☐ Folding chairs
- ☐ Utensils for cooking
- ☐ Bug spray

We're going to Wyoming, so I add a few more items:

- ☐ Bear spray
- ☐ Hats and gloves
- ☐ Rope
- ☐ Pocketknife
- ☐ Hatchet
- ☐ Flashlights
- ☐ Fire-starting kit

I notice Sadie is tapping her chin with her pen.

"Let me see your list." As I reach for it, she quickly swoops it away.

"Only if I can see yours."

"Fine." We trade papers. I study Sadie's short list.

- ☐ Marshmallows
- ☐ Jar for catching bugs
- ☐ Fishing pole
- ☐ Pillow
- ☐ Teddy

One side of my mouth pulls back as I hold in a snort of laughter. Mom's been all over me lately to use kind words. So all I say is, "The fishing poles are a great idea."

We trade back as we pull into the parking lot. After looking both ways, I rush forward to hold the door open for everyone.

Mom mutters as she steps into the store, "Oh, boy, I'm in way over my head."

It's okay. She'll see. Camping is going to be awesome. I'll work double time to make sure she's comfortable. Dad and I compare tent features for so long that Mom and Sadie finally wander off. I pull the box off the shelf and think I might burst. *This is my tent.*

"Let's go find the girls," Dad says.

They're in the sleeping bag section, and Sadie has a pink and purple one with a unicorn horn clutched in her arms.

"We need to get Mom a good bedroll too," I mutter. *Her comfort is at the top of my list.*

Mom's brows lift. "I like the sound of that."

Later when I double-check my list, Mom makes me add up our items. "And…we're over our budget by $25."

I frown at the huge pile of gear in our cart, unwilling to put anything back, except for the unicorn sleeping bag.

"What if I were to use my chore money to cover the rest?"

Dad looks at me. "Seriously? You sure? You've been saving for a four-wheeler all summer."

"And I'm not even close to having enough for one. Besides, I've been dreaming of camping for years. I'm far more committed to this." I push all of Dad's buttons that I can, waving my hand over the pile.

Dad checks his watch. "All right, then. We've got to get home and pack. We'll hit the road at 4:30 a.m. tomorrow. We've got to get Ethan by 5 a.m. if we hope to make it to Grand Teton by Friday."

The name of the park sends a shiver down my spine. *A wilderness where anything could happen.* Dad and I repack his Ford F-250 three times before we fit everything under the cover on the back and snap it down to the bed. I don't sleep a wink that night. I keep running over the items that I packed in my backpack.

- ☑ Knife from Poppa
- ☑ Coil of rope
- ☑ Flashlight
- ☑ Small wire saw
- ☑ Water bottle
- ☑ Power bars
- ☑ Hatchet

A folding shovel is the biggest item I have in my

backpack. I click on the flashlight and flip open my wilderness survival guide. "Ugh." I had nearly forgotten my compass. I add it to my pack, plus my winter hat. Then I tuck my field guide on top.

I chase sleep around all night without catching it even once. I hear Dad coming long before he reaches my bed.

"Is it time to go?" I ask.

He laughs. "Guess you didn't sleep much. I didn't either. I haven't gone camping in years."

We settle into the truck, and I lean on my backpack sitting on my lap. Sadie curls on her side and throws a blanket over her head. *How can she possibly sleep at a time like this?*

When we pull into Ethan's town, Dad's eyes catch mine in the rearview. "Isaiah, I want you to understand something. Ethan may not be his usual self. Aunt Sylvia and Uncle Jim said they have been having some trouble with him."

"*What?*" Sadie whips the blanket off her head. I guess she wasn't quite asleep after all.

"What kind of trouble, Dad?"

He frowns. "Well, I guess he's got some friends who aren't doing him any good. He's got a lot on his mind right now, and that's part of the reason he's coming—to give them a break and get him out of his usual routine."

Sadie bites her lip, and I inch my pack closer to my chest.

"So," Mom adds, "we're going to love him this week and be patient if he isn't quite the cousin you remember from last summer."

We pull into his driveway, and I stare wide-eyed as he hugs Aunt Sylvia. He's a little taller than she is! He trudges toward the truck with his gear. Sadie slides into the middle seat as Ethan hops in. But he's grinning, and his hand is out for a fist bump. Suddenly, everything is normal again.

"Tetons, watch out! The Rawlings are coming!" he says as I hit his fist. All my nerves drain away. *He seems fine—the same fun-loving, sometimes too daring, oldest cousin in our family.*

Aunt Sylvia rushes from the porch and opens Ethan's door to hug him one last time, her eyes full of tears. "Greg," she says to Dad, "don't let him eat any pickles."

She turns to Ethan. "Be safe."

We settle in for two solid days of driving. The miles seem to stretch on forever. *Past forever.* I've re-read my field guide three times, and my shoulder is sore from playing punch bug with Sadie and Ethan. But the landscape outside the window has changed, and now wide, open plains with little sagebrush plants stick up everywhere in the mountains. In the distance, they are sharp and snowcapped. We're seeing more and more wild animals too. Pronghorn race at almost sixty miles an hour next to the truck, and the occasional bugles of majestic elk with huge antlers echo off the mountains.

Sadie sighs, then draws a big breath. I cut in and say, "If you're going to ask if we're there yet, we're not."

When we finally see the huge wooden posts of

a sign that says, "Welcome to Wyoming, Forever West," we all shout.

Dad pulls over so we can take a picture under the sign. Ethan puts two fingers up behind my head, so I tackle him. We quickly make a discovery. Sharp, tiny balls of thorns are scattered all over the ground.

"All right," Mom calls. "Load up."

I pick the nasty little thorns off my shirt as I turn, gazing across the vast expanse of flatland. The great Teton Mountains point skyward like the jagged teeth of a dinosaur. *What adventures await us there?*

-2-

"Look! Jackson Hole! We're here!" Sadie shouts in my ear.

"Not really," I grump. "We're not in the park yet."

"Close enough! Oh, a rodeo? Can we go?" She's pointing to a billboard with a man clinging to the back of a bucking bull. I read the details as Sadie leans over me, trying to see as we pass under the sign.

"Ouch, Sadie, you're elbowing my spleen!"

"Ugh!" she says, "I was just trying to see."

"Listen," Mom says, "we've all been in the car for a long time." She cringes, rubbing her thighs.

"A *really* long time. Let's hold it together for a bit longer. The rodeo starts our last day here; I think it sounds like a great way to end our trip."

"Yeah!" Sadie throws her hands in the air, knocking my bottle of water from the holder and down over my legs.

I stare straight ahead, clenching my teeth. A thousand reactions race through my mind. I cut them off before they jump from my mouth.

"Sorry," Sadie whispers.

"Maybe I could get a paper towel?" I say through my clenched teeth, feeling red creep up my neck. Mom hands the roll back to me with a look of pride in her eyes.

Ethan says, "At least you didn't freak out because there's no way you'd make it through the week in the Tetons if that got to you."

His words make me let go of the anger. "Right. We're tough guys now!"

"What do you say, Isaiah? Should we try a swim in the icy-cold Jenny Lake?"

"I'm game if you are," I boast, determined not to be outdone by my older cousin.

"There it is!" Mom points at the huge sign that reads Grand Teton National Park. I'm not sure if she's really excited at being here, or just that we're almost done driving.

"Let's get a picture, Greg. Pull over, Honey."

Everything is glistening wet; we must have just missed a storm. We pile out of the truck, and Sadie and I race around the sign. She beats me as usual; and Ethan catches my arm, trying to get me in a headlock. We wrestle until Mom's got the camera positioned just so on the hood of the car.

"Okay! Line up; five seconds till it goes off." She hurries forward as we squeeze together, arms around each other.

"Smile," Mom says through her teeth. I look up at the camera but don't consider breaking my rule about never smiling for a picture. Then everything else fades away. There, not 40 yards in front of me, a massive black wolf stares right at me from the shelter of the forest. His golden eyes seem to look right into my soul. I gasp, my finger pointing of its own accord. The flash of the camera goes off.

"Did…" I blink, and he's gone. "Did you see it?" I shriek.

"See what?" Dad asks.

"Wolf! Right there in the trees."

"Where?" Sadie is searching desperately. But he's like a shadow of the forest—somehow meant for my eyes only.

"Must be seeing things," Ethan says, swiping my hair the wrong way.

"No, he was there!" I protest, mashing my hair flat again.

"How do you know this 'wolf' wasn't a she?" Ethan makes quotes with his fingers around the word *wolf.*

Mom scans the tree line with a frown. "Let's get into the park and get settled."

Still, I press my nose against the cold window, searching for those mesmerizing golden eyes.

Dad slows at the admission gate. Before the attendant lets us through, she asks, "Did you bring a bear canister?"

"A what?" Dad asks.

The lady smiles, pointing at the map of the park. "You'll need to go straight to the Jenny Lake Store. All campers are required to use bear canisters for their food. We have plenty of both brown and black bears in the park and keeping your food out of their way is very important."

"All right, thanks," Dad replies.

The awe of seeing the wolf still grips me. Before we've gone a mile down the winding road, I've spotted twelve elk, a bald eagle, seven turkeys, and what Sadie insists was a brown bear but was actually a reddish-colored boulder.

The drive to the store takes nearly 45 minutes,

but the time flies by as I stare at the incredible snowcapped peaks. They're so narrow and sharp at the tip it seems like you could prick your finger on the summit—if you could get that high.

I keep catching glimpses of a black streak racing through the pines. I tell myself it's just my imagination. *Maybe.* I groan as I get out of the truck at the lodge, my legs cramping from the long days in the car.

The store and visitors' center are built of log and set in front of a crystal-clear lake that perfectly reflects the mountains and pine trees. While Mom and Dad decide what size bear canister we need to purchase, Ethan, Sadie, and I walk around through the aisles.

Ethan picks up a multi-tool. "These are the best brand! My dad has one." A shadow passes over his face. Sadie and I look at each other, wondering how to help him.

"Oh, look! It also has a fire starter built in." I point to the package, hoping to distract him. But he's already hanging it up with the rest. We follow him around the next turn.

A group of four teenage boys huddle near the cooler section. They're all wearing cowboy hats and belts with huge buckles. Their height reminds me of Max at school. I suppress a shiver of dread, pushing him out of my mind.

I catch the tallest one's harsh voice as he snarls, "Well, she won't win this year. I'll make sure of it."

The other boys snicker and nod. The one who'd spoken scowls at us, and the rest of the group does the same. I'm already shifting to turn down the closest aisle, but Ethan saunters up to them, his chest out. He's nearly as tall as they are, and he points to the cooler behind them. "Excuse me, I need to get a drink."

Sadie inches behind me; she's shy sometimes, and the look the boys are leveling at Ethan is far from friendly. The stare down lasts a few more seconds that seem longer than the drive to Wyoming. Finally, the boys move off.

"Tourist." The tallest one spits the word.

"What did you say?" Ethan asks.

"You heard me," the boy says over his shoulder as he leads the group out of the store.

"Ethan!" Sadie hisses, while he grabs a soda. "Why did you mess with those guys? They give me the creeps."

Ethan shrugs. "They don't own the place."

He's grown a lot more than just taller. I wish I could face Max with the same confidence that Ethan has.

Sadie elbows me. "Can we get sodas?"

"Sadie, you know you and sugar are dangerous together," I say with a straight face, but remembering the trouble she got into last time she ate a candy bar makes me smile. I taunt her, "Two broken dishes, plus Mom's vase. I don't think Grand Teton is quite ready for how crazy you get on sugar."

"Isaiah…" she whines my name for bringing up that incident, her face red.

"Come on, y'all!" Mom calls, "Let's get to site

A-68! Oh, do you think we should grab some firewood?"

As Ethan heads toward the cashier to pay for his soda, Dad responds, "No. We're allowed to pick up wood at the campsite."

-3-

Back in the truck, Sadie studies the park map. "Why do we have to stay in a campground called *Gross Venture?* What an awful name!"

Mom holds back a chuckle. "No, sweetie. *Gros Ventre* is pronounced like saying 'grow Vaughn.' *Gros Ventre* is a French name meaning 'white clay people,' and the pronunciation of their words doesn't follow our normal rules."

"Well, I hope the bears follow the rules and come to check out our new canister."

"It's to keep the bears *away* from smelling our food, honey—not to bring them closer."

"Aw, bummer."

"Can you find our site on the map? We should be the farthest site on the farthest loop."

"Here it is, right by the river! We might see moose!"

When I step out at the site, a thrill runs up my legs. Seven days of wilderness bliss here is a dream come true. I rush to the tailgate and haul out the tent for Ethan and me. We get it spread out, and while we're trying to figure out the poles, Sadie hops by, tucked deep inside her purple unicorn sleeping bag. She looks like she's in a sack race, with only her face showing. Her wild jumps force the flopping unicorn to cover her eyes. She's giggling and leaping, and she twists straight into our tangle of poles and canvas.

"Sadie!" I shout as poles fly everywhere.

She peeks out from under the unicorn like a giant purple inchworm. "Oops."

Mom comes around the truck with the box in her hands. "Sadie, don't jump around in the dirt in your sleeping bag. Come and help me."

By the time Ethan and I get our tent together, the sun is sinking low in the sky.

"I'm hungry," I say for the twelfth time.

"Me too," Mom replies. "Why don't you kids go collect some wood, and we'll cook the burgers."

Ethan and I race to fill our arms first, but the only wood around here is more like twigs. Correction. Make that wet twigs! My sleeves are soaked through by the time I dump my load next to the metal fire ring. The temperature is dropping fast, and I'm sure looking forward to a crackling fire and a juicy, smoky burger.

"Dad, I think every camper here for the last 40 years has gathered firewood from those woods."

He frowns at our nearly dripping lump of thin branches. We gather around the fire ring, and watch Dad get the smallest twigs set up like a teepee, and I pull out my ferro rod. I've been itching to use it since the shopping trip. I run my finger down the rod of rough metal. I've watched plenty of videos on how to use a kit like this. Confidently, I pull out the striker and run it down the length of the rod. Sparks fly like crazy, making me jump back. Still, I have to scrape it harder than I thought I would, and soon my hands are trembling from the effort.

"Um. Shouldn't something be happening?" I ask. Glancing over at Ethan, I find he's not faring any better with his striker. I grit my teeth and scrape harder.

Dad is using a magnesium starter kit, which requires him to shave slivers off a silver rectangle of metal. He gathers up a rather impressive pile of metal shavings, then strikes the other side of the shaver against the magnesium, and it flares into bright flames under the damp twig teepee.

I've never seen metal burn before, and I stare at it, mesmerized.

One lazy curl of smoke rises; then the magnesium burns out. Dad squats by the cold fire ring and frowns. "I imagined that going better than it did."

Ethan and I combine our efforts, but the twigs refuse to even smoke for us.

"Um, Dad? Did you bring any lighter fluid?" I ask, belly growling loudly.

"We were going old school, remember? Doing real-man stuff." Dad struggles with the wet wood, and I head toward the river to see if I can find anything drier.

"Stay where we can see you from the tents," Mom calls after me.

"Sure, Mom," I holler, stepping into the shelter of some scrubby pines.

Up ahead, I see a flicker of motion and freeze, searching for what made it.

There! It's a female elk near the riverbank. She bounds away, and I look down at the sandy soil before me.

I see a print a few yards ahead. I kneel next to it reverently, remembering details from my tracking game book. With four toe pads and one large main pad plus claw marks, it's definitely some sort of canine. I spread my hand over it, finding the print larger than my palm. That's when I know it's a wolf print.

A shiver runs across my chest, remembering those deep golden eyes. I scan the trees, then make quick work of the trek back to camp. Dad hasn't made any progress.

"Honey? Everybody's hungry. How about peanut butter and jelly sandwiches for tonight?"

"Burgers would be better," I say, one hand over my stomach.

"Maybe sandwiches are a good idea," Dad says as he adjusts the twigs for the hundredth time. Mom digs in the cooler, and I sure don't like the look on her face when she pulls out the bread. It's smashed flat on one end and dripping water.

"Oh, no!" she says.

Ethan, Sadie, and I gather around.

"Ewww," Sadie says, one side of her nose wrinkling up.

Eventually we settle for cheese and crackers and power bars for supper, eaten around our sad cold firepit.

Trying to rally our spirits, Mom says, "So...what

are each of you looking forward to at school this new year?"

Her words make me freeze, my mouth dry.

Ethan shifts on the rocks he's balancing on. "I'm trying out for quarterback of our football team this year."

"Seeing Laura! And gym class and math," Sadie says easily.

"Isaiah, what about you?" Mom says.

I swallow hard and stare at the wet wood.

"You look like you saw a ghost or something," Sadie adds.

I see only one thing at school—Max Smith. By the end of last year, I'd barely been able to get myself to face him each day. Max should've been grades above me, out of middle school already, but he'd been held back twice to remain the terror of Stanford Middle School.

"Honey? Are you all right?" The concern in Mom's voice forces me toward effort.

"I...I...Max... I mean, I guess science might

be cool." *It's the only class Max won't be in. I wish I could just disappear.*

"Max?" Sadie says. "Is that the kid who hates you?"

I stare at her blankly, my insides shriveling as Max's insults from last year pound me.

Ethan stuffs a bite of a power bar into his mouth. "You want me to scare him for you?"

I shake my head, voice cracking. "No. It's something I have to deal with on my own."

-4-

My eyes drift open slowly, and I scowl at a curl of frosted breath rising from my face. *Camping! The Grand Tetons await!* I ease out of my sleeping bag, their outlines barely visible with dawn just thinking about appearing.

Ethan is still fast asleep, a string of drool hanging from his open mouth. I pull on my boots and coat. The tent material crinkles as I try to remember my dream.

I unzip the tent just enough to slip out, and my dream comes back to me. Dad and I had been trying to get the fire going. We were hunched over in the cold, flames refusing to form. Then, from the side, a huge shadow had fallen over us, crisply outlining the shape of a fat man with jiggling rolls hanging everywhere. But when I looked up, no one was there!

Then everything shifted, and Ethan was standing next to me, stuffing gummy worms up his nose. I don't think that part of the dream was important, though. *Fat.* That's the word that's been sticking in my mind all night. Finally, it comes to me. *Fatwood!* That's what we need to find to start our fire.

I grab my hatchet and survival guide, flipping pages as I walk toward the pines near the river. On page 35, I find the directions for hunting fatwood.

Step one. Look for a dead pine tree still standing.

Step two. Find places in the tree where the wood "changes direction," such as where a branch intersects the trunk.

Step three. Cut off the branch as close to

the tree trunk as possible. Check the cut end for darker stains in the wood—purplish or red streaks. These stains contain a very flammable resin that has collected called fatwood. The fatwood also has a strong smell of pine.

Step four. Shave the fatwood into small chips and then light them with the ferro rod.

I enter the patch of trees, noting its strange emptiness—no birds, deer, or even a squirrel. *Maybe these early morning hours have them all so quiet.* I spy the outline of a dead pine tree straight ahead. Rubbing my hands together, I long for the warmth of a fire in this bitter cold air.

Right before I swing my hatchet, my hair stands on end, and I turn slowly to scan the woods. I flinch when I spot one golden eye peering out from behind a tree. The black wolf is even bigger this close!

Every nerve is on fire as I stare back at him, gripping my weapon. *Do wolves hunt 12-year-old boys?*

- 5 -

I blink, and he's gone—just a flash of coarse black fur fading into the trees.

My hand trembles as I grip the branch beside me. *I'm thankful he wasn't interested in a breakfast composed of Isaiah—at least for now.* Still, I know something is different inside of me from seeing him. I feel stronger and better because he was there.

I swing the hatchet, driving it into the wood and shaking out the trembling feeling of too much adrenaline at seeing the wolf. Felling the low branch takes much longer than I had planned. Eagerly I pick up the branch and look for the fatwood. I see a streak of purplish wood in the cut end!

If I hurry, I can get a hot cup of coffee ready for Mom before she's awake.

I didn't think shaving this branch would be as hard a task as I find it to be. *Maybe if I cut the branch into shorter pieces and then stand one on end?* Hunkering down, I try my idea. Working hard, I fall into a steady rhythm of strokes with a nice pile of chips growing around the stick.

I gather them in my pockets and jog back to camp. Glancing over my shoulder for the wolf, I find the sun is still thinking about coming over the sharp faces of the Tetons.

"Hurry!" I mutter. After last night's complete fire failure, I've got to make this camping trip better for Mom, or she'll never agree to do it again.

I grin widely as the chips ignite with only one firm downward stroke on my ferro rod. I choose the driest twigs from last night and settle them over the flaming chips.

I've done it! The flames are crackling now, and I must sort of toss in the wood because the heat is too intense. I leave plenty of space for air between the wood, poking it with another stick.

Carefully, I set the cooking grate over the fire ring and run to fill the small kettle that had come with our cooking kit. I hunch close to the warmth, seeing the wolf's eyes in the flames. Soon, I see steam rising from the kettle, and the sun's rays reveal the incredible beauty and splendor of the Teton Mountains.

"Wow!" I whisper, deciding that sunrise might be my favorite time of day. When I hear rustling within Mom's and Dad's tent, I rush for a mug and desperately search the label of the instant coffee. *How much for one cup?* No time for a measuring spoon, so I just dump some into the bottom of her cup and then pour in hot water as she steps out of her tent.

"Good morning, Mom!" I greet her, handing her the steaming cup. "Did you sleep good?" I ask, knowing my entire camping future hinges on her answer.

She takes the cup with an amazed expression and sniffs the coffee until her eyelids flutter with delight.

"Yes, actually, I slept really well." She looks around the camp. "Did you start this fire all by yourself?" The admiration in her eyes makes all the effort worth it.

"I remembered a trick to start fires."

"Well, I wish I could remember things like that. Hey! You know, with this awesome fire, we can make stick bread for breakfast. I've been so excited to try it ever since I saw the recipe online."

Soon, everyone is nibbling hot cinnamon bread warmed by our pine sticks. I still can't believe I'd struck the fire all by myself.

"Let's head up to Jenny Lake and take a hike today," Dad says, taking Mom's hand in his. *I guess we're both eager for her to enjoy camping.*

The day passes quickly in a blur of pure wilderness bliss, complete with elk and bison sightings, hiking, exploring the Jenny Lake Visitor Center with its 3-D maps, and gathering more wood with Sadie and Ethan.

By the time I hit my sleeping bag, everything catches up with me, and I'm asleep before I can mumble good night to Ethan.

I dream of a fierce race between the creatures of the Grand Tetons. The black wolf runs behind the herds of deer and pronghorn until the keen light in his eyes grows even brighter, and he snaps at the heels of the slowest runners. The ground shakes from the pounding of their hooves.

"Isaiah!" a worried voice intrudes, but I have to know if the wolf catches one of the deer. "Isaiah!" Ethan is shaking my shoulder hard, making the tent crinkle under me. "What is that?" he shouts point-blank in my ear.

Wide awake now, I find the ground is still trembling, and a deep pounding thunders in my chest.

-6-

"I don't know!" I shout, leaping for the tent zipper. Ethan and I stumble into the dim moonlight, and the eerie howl of a lone wolf makes my blood run like ice. Huge dark shadows are rushing in our direction, charging up the slight incline to our site.

"Move!" I roar at Ethan, who stands still, mouth open, staring at the stampede bearing down on us. I shove him hard toward the picnic table right in front of the other tent where Mom, Dad, and Sadie are sleeping.

A heartbeat later, the shadows materialize into shining hooves and bright eyes glistening in the moonlight. The first dark figure smashes straight into our empty tent, spitting gravel as his massive bulk bucks and twists at the sudden contact. I hear the tent poles snap over the heaving breath of the buffalo.

The herd splits around the picnic table, Sadie is screaming inside their tent behind us, and Ethan and I hunker down, covering our heads. Choking dust flies everywhere, and stones hit me like the sting of 100 bees.

Someone is shouting. Finally, I realize it's me, and I shut my mouth as the last straggling animal careens through the camp. Mom emerges, face frightened, clutching Sadie in her arms.

"What's happening?" she shouts. Dad comes through the tent opening right behind them, his eyes on our smashed tent now crumpled in the distance. Making out details in the moonlight is difficult.

"Isaiah! Ethan!" he shouts, his voice pinched.

"Right here, Dad." My voice comes out smooth

in the dark—so close it makes Sadie giggle. Dad lets out a huge breath and wraps us both in a bear hug. *He's trembling.*

"We're fine, Dad. Ethan woke me up just in time." I wipe my eyes, my heart full and overflowing at his concern. "This picnic table saved our entire family."

"Was it buffalo?" he asks.

"I think so. It was too dark to see, really, but they were big enough, that's for sure."

"I'm so thankful everyone's all right. Let's see if we can get your tent back together."

"You think everyone else is all right?" Sadie's face is pale as she searches in the direction of the rest of the campground.

"I think the herd veered toward the left—away from the rest of the campsites," Ethan answers as we wrestle with the flopping tent.

"Oh, dear," Dad says, as he lifts the limp tent fabric with poles sticking out here and there.

"Here, Dad. We can tape sticks to the parts that

aren't broken like splints. It will be all right," I say. My voice is far more confident than I feel inside.

"Great idea," Dad says.

I rush for the tape in his truck, but it's nearly dawn before Ethan and I lie back down in our now-crooked tent. I'm wide awake, all my nerves still tingling.

"Ethan? Thanks," I say, imagining what it would have been like inside as the animals ran over the tent.

"Sure. No problem. Whenever you need saving, just call me," he adds lightly.

No way is either of us going to go back to sleep. "Did you hear the wolf howl right before the herd overran our camping site?"

"I guess I did. It's all kind of a blur in my mind. One thing's for sure though, I'd like to know what spooked them so bad."

"Yeah, me too. Maybe we can follow the tracks in the morning and figure it out."

-7-

We talk until the sun is up, its warmth creeping into the rocks all around. Dad agrees to hike out with us to see where the herd had come from while Mom makes breakfast.

I grab my tracking game guidebook and study the hoofprints. Sadie's face is still a little pale, and I want to see her smile come back.

"Sadie, do you think these are a match?" I point at the buffalo print drawn on the page.

She takes the book, frowning as she studies it and then the ground. "No. I don't think they are. See, the buffalo prints in the book have a sharper edge, and they curl more at the toe. They look more like deer prints than these."

I looked down to find she's right. "So, maybe they're just cows and not buffalo?"

The light is back in her eyes now. "I think so. How far do you think they ran?"

Ethan answers as he tops the first rise. "Not far."

We hurry to catch up; from the hilltop, I can see for miles. The terrain is a mix of rocky red ground, patches of sagebrush and grass. I also see a sturdy barbed-wire fence.

"I thought there weren't any fences in a national park?" Sadie puts her hands on her hips.

"Well, actually our campground is at the eastern edge of the park," Dad says, striding down the hill. "Come on, let's see if we can uncover what made the animals stampede."

The fence was farther than it looked. When we finally reach it, Dad says, "Be careful not to step on any prints; stay to the side so we can read everything."

We edge up to examine the broken strands of wire.

"That stampede was definitely cattle," I say. "The ground in the fence's corner is turned up like the herd had bunched up there for a while before bursting through."

"Shoot," Ethan says. "Being nearly squashed by a herd of stampeding buffalo sounds way cooler."

"Look at this!" Sadie exclaims, pointing at the ground.

Right on top of the freshly turned dirt at the broken fence line is a clear line of distinctly different prints.

"Dog or wolf?" Sadie asks, digging in her pack.

I pull out the tracking book again. "It says here that wolf's prints are usually five inches by four inches, much larger than a dog's, and they should single track, meaning the print from the hind paws should be right on top of the front prints." I scan further in the book. "Dogs usually have a wider chest, so their prints don't line up like a wolf." I kneel next to the tracks, touching one reverently, remembering the wild howl. *Had he been hunting the cows?*

Sadie's got her new plaster casting kit out, pouring water from her canteen into the thick white powder.

Dad wanders down to a small stream nearby, but Ethan points just within the broken fence. "Look at that!"

"So what? It's only a boot print. I'm sure the rancher comes out here plenty," I say, looking at the deep tread marks.

"No, listen. The prints are on top of the cattle prints in some places and underneath in others. That means someone was here during and after the cows' little dancing act."

I scowl. *He's right; and deep in my gut, that feeling drifts up.* It's the one I get right before I crash my bike trying a new trick, or when without seeing Max, I know he's right behind me.

"Sadie, get a cast of this boot print too, will you please?"

"On it," she says, "I just finished pouring plaster into the wolf print. Oh, no, I may have mixed too much." She's still got half a jug of wet plaster. "Anything else we should cast?"

"Yeah, how about a cow track, and this…" Ethan

squats down pointing, and I jump the fresh tracks to join him. Here and there, under the jumble of animal prints, I make out the tread of a four-wheeler tire.

I rub my chin. "So, first there was an ATV or four-wheeler, then came the herd, then came the wolf. Plus, a man was running around in there somewhere."

Sadie dumps the rest of the plaster into the tire marks. Something bright catches my eye. The broken fencing wire lies in wild curls smashed into the dirt in some places. But on a long arch of it, stuck to a sharp barb, is a small bit of red.

On closer inspection, it's a shred of a red flannel shirt. I tuck it into my coat pocket, as something reflects the sunlight right below where the fabric was. I reach down and pick up a bright new #10 nail. I tuck it in my pocket, and Sadie digs at the wolf cast, popping it up, brushing off the dirt as she inspects it.

"Yes!" she squeals with delight.

"Good one, Sadie," Ethan says, admiring the perfect imprint.

Dad walks back from exploring. "Come on. Mom will be worried if we stay out too much longer."

"Wait, Dad, I've got to get these other imprints." Sadie works quickly, handing me the heavy boot cast. Ethan gets the four-wheeler tracks, and Sadie carries the wolf cast reverently back to camp.

I study the plaster in my hands as we trudge back up the hill. The tread on the outside of the heel is worn almost off. I twist my feet, trying to get my boot to strike the ground with the outside part of my heel first. My toes stick way out when I do, and I have to sort of shuffle. *I bet that's just how the person who made these prints walks.*

"Listen!" Dad stops, his head cocked.

- 8 -

"Hoofbeats," I respond, the sound all too familiar to me. We turn to see what looks like a posse of five figures on horseback, galloping through the broken fence, obliterating the tracks from the mystery stampede.

The horses reach us quicker than I would've thought, and a tough-looking man in a cowboy hat reins his horse to a halt next to us. Swinging off his mount, he greets us. "Morning to you. Did y'all see my cattle?"

"Sure thing. Around midnight they ran right over my son's tent."

A worried look immediately crosses the man's

face. "Was anybody hurt in that stampede through your camp?"

"Thank the Lord, no. The boys heard them coming and got out in time," Dad answers. He grips Ethan's shoulder.

"Glad to hear it. Never had any trouble out of this herd before, and I'm extra careful to keep fences on the park side in good condition."

Sadie, Ethan, and I exchange glances. *There's more to the story, I just know it.*

The man tips his hat, walks forward to a flat spot, then swings up onto his horse, and spurs away. The others follow, except one pale yellow horse with a white mane and tail. Its rider holds back the prancing horse easily; the rider can't be any older than Ethan. Dad follows the horses to the top of the rise, watching over Mom at the campsite.

"Hello, I'm Julie," the rider says.

"Hey," Sadie and I say together. Ethan is strangely quiet.

"I'm glad you're all right. Cattle stampedes can

cause real damage. Did you happen to see which way the herd went?"

I shrug. "It was pretty dark, but Ethan might know."

Ethan just shrugs, his hands deep in his pockets, staring up at Julie as she adjusts her hat.

Sadie steps toward the horse. "Can I pet him?"

"Only if you tell me your name," Julie says teasingly.

"I'm Sadie, and that's my brother Isaiah. What's your horse's name?" she asks, rubbing his glistening neck.

"Timber. He's my barrel horse—the fastest one in Wyoming. What's that you got there?" she asks as she points at the bright-white cast in Sadie's hands.

"It's a cast of a wolf print I made down near the broken fence."

"Wolf. Daddy won't like the sounds of that. Was it mixed right in with the cattle?"

"Actually, it was on top of their tracks."

Julie purses her lips. "It's strange though; this is a herd of heifers—cows that haven't given birth yet. The wolves usually only go after small calves, especially in the summer when the cold isn't driving them."

"I don't think it was the wolf's fault," I blurt out, realizing how ridiculous that sounds. But deep inside, I can't believe that the black wolf was the culprit. *His howl had sounded far off that night, yet his prints are right there.*

"Well, it was nice to meet y'all. I'd better catch up with Daddy."

Sadie steps back from the horse, and Timber launches forward like he was shot out of a cannon.

"Wow!" Sadie whispers.

I bump Ethan with my elbow. "Cat got your tongue?"

His face reddens, and he jams his hands farther into his pockets. "Didn't have anything to say."

"Sure." I don't believe him one bit.

-9-

The sun hovers straight up; I wipe sweat off my nose after jumping a small creek. "I need a break."

"Me too," Sadie pants.

"Sure, we can stop for you young'uns—especially you, Isaiah, loaded down with all that gear. What do you have, like 20 pounds of stuff in your pockets?" Ethan says, but the way he flops onto the log tells me he's tired too.

"Look at that view," Mom says, staring out at the mountains all around.

I step up closer and hug her with one arm. "Mom. Thanks for letting us camp."

She slips her arm around me, smiling. "I have

to admit, I wasn't thrilled about the idea. But there is something about being here, isn't there? Reconnecting with creation."

Ethan groans, stretching his legs. "This place looks like that scene from one of those movie where the dinosaurs take over the world. It's really weirding me out."

We've been hiking for a few hours now and have only made it halfway.

"What's that sound?" he questions.

I must admit that Ethan has good ears.

Ethan shoots to his feet, eyes wide. "It's thudding just like the...the..." He's pointing with a trembling finger at the forest, and something is coming this way through the brush. But Ethan is in another place, terrified.

"Velociraptor!" he screeches, taking off down the trail like an Olympic sprinter. "Everybody run!" he shouts over his shoulder.

"Ethan!" Dad shouts after him, but he dives off the path and into the brush.

"Honey," Mom says, "you'd better go catch him before he runs all the way to Jackson Hole!"

I didn't know Dad could still move that fast. Deciding where to look is hard—at Dad's impressive sprint or the crashing approach of something in the woods.

Sadie giggles as a cow sticks its head through the brush. Its ears look like radar scanners. "Some velociraptor!"

The cow squeezes past and trots to the stream for a drink. Julie rides Timber at an easy walk behind it until the horse is on the trail next to us.

"Hello again," she says, but this time she's much more disheveled and has a twig stuck in her hair.

"Hi, Julie! Looks like you found one cow at least," Sadie says, wasting no time in stepping up to pat Timber's nose.

"This is the last one, actually. Daddy and the boys rounded up all the others. This one's got a screw loose in her brain somewhere, and she wouldn't stay with the herd, so she's our job—Timber's and mine." Julie pats her horse's neck, smiling. "Where's Ethan?"

I look down the trail, nearly telling her the velociraptor story, but he had saved me from being pulverized last night, so I cut off Sadie. "He'll be back in a second."

Sure enough, he and Dad step out of the brush, still panting hard. His face jumps a shade redder as he catches sight of Julie, leaning her elbow easily on the saddle horn.

"Oh. Um. Hey."

I think it's an impressive string of words, considering his inability to speak to her before.

"Were you running?" Julie asks, smiling wide.

"It's...um..." Ethan shrugs. "Exercise is good for everybody."

Dad looks at Ethan out of the corner of his eye. *But I haven't been able to get the wolf off my mind. What if we had brought trouble on him by telling Julie he was there?*

"You think your dad will blame the wolf?"

She shrugs. "Hard to say. They've certainly caused trouble before, and it didn't end well for the wolves. A full pack could take down a grown cow if they were hungry enough. But, right now, I've got to get this platter of beef off park land as quickly as possible. We shouldn't be in the park."

I can't see her tell Timber to step forward, but the horse does at some invisible signal. *Must be mind control.* She stops again.

"Oh, do y'all know about the rodeo on Friday? Old Timber and I will take a stab at the fastest time on the cloverleaf barrels." She bites her lip, nerves showing through. "If I can take first place in calf roping and the ranchers' class and score pretty good on barrels, I'll be the high point youth rider of the year. I've just got to beat Cindy fair and square."

"Wow! Will you ride Timber for all the classes?" Sadie asks.

"No, I have two other horses, and I'll need all of them to win. They each have specific training." As she turns to leave, she waves, mostly at Ethan. And the cow with a mind of her own takes off into the brush ahead of Timber.

"Three horses…" Sadie whispers longingly.

"Don't get any ideas," Dad says to her.

"Too late," she replies.

-10-

"Where's my knife?" I ask, patting my pockets.

Pulling on a bright yellow hoodie, Ethan gives me a look. "Maybe it's under the air mattress or in your back pocket," he teases.

"No. Seriously. I can't find it."

"You mean the one Poppa gave you?" Sadie asks, knowing how important the knife is to me. Unable to say it, I just nod at her. "Okay, Isaiah. Think, when did you last have it?" she asks, her face full of concern.

"This morning, before the hike, I clipped it right here to my pocket." I pat the right side of my pants, which admittedly jingles with a mini ferro rod, an emergency fishing hook and line, a handful of fat woodchips, and the nail I'd picked up at the fence.

Sadie frowns at my pocket like it's a suspect. "I'll go check in the truck. Maybe it came off your pocket when you sat down."

"Thanks," I mumble. *My sister is great for a girl.* Even Ethan catches the heaviness of my loss, and he helps me search the tent. I adjust the coil of rope I have slung across my chest as Sadie comes back from the truck.

"Nothing." She didn't need to say it; I can read it on her face.

Mom comes over to wrap an arm around my shoulders. "It might turn up yet, Isaiah. Did you think to pray?"

"Okay, Mom. I will," I answer, staring at the ground, fighting back tears. Poppa had passed that knife onto me; it had been his dad's. I feel like I had lost a part of our family.

"Here." Mom holds out baked potatoes fresh off the campfire and says, "Why don't you three go explore the Gros Ventre River? Another camper said the river is higher than she's ever seen it though, so stay away from the water." She checks her watch. "Try to be back here in an hour, all right?"

Ethan inhales his potato in three bites and sets off. Sadie takes mine and hers from Mom. "Come on, Bud. let's go exploring."

I take the warm, buttery potato she hands me and force some down, but I still can't shake off the loss. Maybe Ethan's trying to cheer me up, or maybe it's just a surge of energy from the free time and a full belly, but he's slipped into a hilarious mood.

"I've started eating clocks..." he says, leaping from boulder to boulder.

"What?" Sadie asks, looking at him like he's absolutely crazy.

"It's quite time-consuming!" He doubles over, slapping his knees. I resist the urge to smile.

"Why can't you hear a pterodactyl in the bathroom?" he asks.

Sadie folds her arms across her chest. "What is it with you and dinosaurs?"

"Give up?" Ethan asks. "Because it has a silent P." He goes off into another fit of laughter.

One laugh escapes, and I think Ethan's mood is infectious. We're nearing the river that's running far below the cliffs where we are standing. The rushing water froths white as it rushes through a tight channel created by the cliffs on both sides.

Right at the edge of the strange red rocks that form the cliffs, Ethan turns theatrically, one finger high in the air.

"Somebody stole my mood ring..." He draws in a breath to finish, but the skittering sound of rocks sliding over each other covers his voice. He wobbles and struggles for balance as the cliff side gives way. Ethan disappears before our eyes!

"Ethan!" I scream, rushing forward. Sadie is running hard too, shouting his name. *I have to stop her before she goes over as well!*

-11-

I dig deep, legs pumping, and catch her elbow right before she plunges onto the loose shale.

"There!" I point downstream where a flash of yellow shows in the whitewater rushing away.

"Ethan!" Sadie calls as we sprint alongside the dangerous cliff, desperate to see him break the surface again.

Skidding down a steep bank of shale, we slide to an area of riverbank that's almost level with the thrashing water. This close, its power is terrifying, and an ice-cold spray catches my cheek as we run beside the river.

"Hurry!" Sadie shrieks, pointing downriver to a place where a log jam makes the water even angrier. *If it sucks him under the logs, he could get caught underneath!*

"No!" I shout aloud at the thought, stripping off the coil of rope as I dodge tree branches.

Tears streak down Sadie's face. "Look! He's caught a root!"

We keep running as I study the frothing water; sure enough, a short way ahead, Ethan is desperately gripping a thin root near a small island in the middle of the river.

"Help!" His wild cry rips at me as I search for a way to save him. The root gives way in a shower of dirt, and the water swallows him again.

Sadie screams, and I cut in front of her. "Sadie, I've got to get ahead of Ethan with the rope."

I lower my head and plow right through the low-hanging branches. "Ethan!" I shout.

His head breaks the surface to my left, and I see him suck in a desperate breath before the river yanks him under again. Spurred by his terrified expression, I run forward, not even feeling the rough terrain. I scoop up a wide piece of driftwood and cinch the end of the rope around it. Ethan appears again, just ahead of me. He makes a crazed grab for a low-hanging branch.

"Yes!" I thunder the word when the branch holds. But the water is searching for a way to pull Ethan under, and I know he can't hold on for long.

"Sadie!"

She's suddenly there at my side, and I hand her the long coil of rope, keeping a few loops and the tied-off piece of driftwood in my hands.

"If I miss, pull it in as fast as you can," I shout, whirling the driftwood like David against Goliath. I let it go and watch the wavering length of rope as it snakes over the water. It splashes, barely visible as the current sweeps it quickly past Ethan.

"Pull it in!"

She's desperately yanking hand over hand, and by the time I'm ready to throw it again, Ethan's grip has slipped to the very tip of the branch.

"Arrgghh!" I roar as I throw, this time far upriver.

"Now!" I shout as the current sucks the driftwood close to Ethan. With a desperate lunge, he lets go of the branch. Everything goes under, and

I almost forget to grip the rope. Suddenly, it yanks tight, pulling Sadie and me closer to the dangerous bank.

We are no match for the ferocious current as Ethan sweeps farther away, bear hugging the wood, his face dunking under.

"Get the end around a tree!" I shriek at Sadie while the rope zings through my hands, burning hotter by the second. "Hurry!" The pain grows so intense I almost drop the rope.

She takes the end and darts around a slim pine trunk. The rope twangs tight, and I desperately hope Ethan held on through the sudden, jolting stop.

"When I pull, you take out the slack and draw it tight around the tree again!" I heave on the rope for all I'm worth. My muscles are burning, but I take hope in the heavy weight on the far end. *He must still be hanging on though I still can't see him.*

Sadie works the rope, keeping it tight as I slowly draw Ethan in.

"Yes! I see him!" Her shout gives me a surge of

wild energy, and I drag him closer. "Pull, Isaiah! You've got this!" She leans hard on the rope, helping all she can.

Ethan flops to shore, shoulders first; and then with one last tug, he's out of the river's grasp.

Sadie is on him in a second, bear-hugging him as he's sprawled on the pine-needled earth.

I crumple to the ground, every muscle shaking, unable to even stand after the intense effort. I crawl on hands and knees over to them and flop next to Ethan. We stare up through the evergreens at the crisp blue sky, just breathing in and out so very glad to be alive—a feeling I've never known so clearly before.

"So," I pant. "What's the punchline?"

"What?" he asks, his voice raspy.

"You said somebody stole your mood ring…"

"Oh, that…" The word comes out with a cough. "Somebody stole my mood ring; now I don't know how I feel about that…or the river."

-12-

Sadie snorts a laugh, and soon we've all joined in. The trembling fades as my muscles return to normal. But I notice Ethan is shivering as his soaked clothes drain cold water. I place a hand on his shoulder, shocked by how cold it is. The realization sets in that he could be suffering from hypothermia. "Let's get you back to camp and into some dry clothes. Can you stand up?" I ask.

He groans, trying to roll over. Sadie pushes and helps get him to a sitting position. "I don't kn... kn...know."

The shivering grips him so hard he can barely get out any words.

There's a green feeling in my stomach. It's not a good sign that his muscles aren't responding. He could still be in deep trouble. "We can't be that far from camp. We don't have a choice, Ethan; you've got to get up."

I quickly recoil the rope and set it across my chest. Then I take his hand, and pain explodes in mine. The rope had burned them far worse than I had thought. Now that the adrenaline is wearing off, the pain is setting in deep. I bite my lip and force Ethan to his feet. With one arm over my shoulder and Sadie at his other side, we're soon all wet and cold.

Stumbling forward, we eventually reach the bottom of the cliff. We stare up at it open-mouthed. It's nearly straight up, with two trails of freshly turned stones from Sadie and me skiing down.

"How did we do that?" Sadie asks.

"Sheer desperation," I respond. Ethan shivers hard again. "But the fact is, there's no possibility that we're going to get back to camp that way."

We're hemmed in by the river on one side and the cliffs ahead, so we trudge to the east, hoping the cliff will level out soon, allowing us to climb back to camp.

Soon the cliff veers hard to the south. I have a sinking feeling that we're getting farther from our goal. The cutting wind races down the cliff's face, and along with his violent shivering, Ethan's lips are turning blue.

"Wait! I've got a survival blanket somewhere."

Ethan tries to stand on his own as I pat my pockets, searching for the thin packet. Finally, I pull it out and rip open the plastic coating. The survival blanket is silver and crinkly. I can't imagine it actually creating any warmth; but I unfold it to a full 4' x 8' section, and Ethan wraps it around himself.

"Look!" Sadie is pointing to a trail that dives into the woods.

I wish I knew what was best to do. *I wish Dad was here with his wide hand on my shoulder. Then everything would be all right.*

"Let's take the trail. We've got to get Ethan out of this wind fast." We turn in, noting that the grass is mashed flat in two wide strips. *Must've been a four-wheeler.* At least the breeze is stilled within the shelter of the trees. As we hobble around a bend, I'm not sure I can support Ethan any longer. He's so much bigger than me, and my knees are about to buckle.

A makeshift camp comes into view, with a rock ring and half-charred wood still in its center; a circle of logs sits around the firepit.

"Let's stop and build a fire. We've got to get you warmed up."

Ethan doesn't respond, and his movements are even clumsier. Sadie helps Ethan stay upright as I kneel by the wood, digging the fat woodchips out of my pocket, almost whimpering as the rope burns sting like crazy.

When I have the wood arranged in a teepee like Dad had made, I strike the ferro rod. The resulting explosion of sparks ignites the chips at the base. I rush into the trees for more fuel, ignoring the pain in my hands. Soon there's heat wafting up.

I dig in my back pocket and find a fruit leather and a stick of beef jerky. We get Ethan's sweatshirt off, and all three of us huddle under the thin but effective silver sheet of the survival blanket. We hunch on the log nearest the fire and absorb its warmth.

"Here, eat something." I pull out the food and hand it to Sadie and Ethan.

"Isaiah, wh…what happened to your hands?" he asks, seeing the bright red marks as he takes the dried meat.

"The rope…" But my words trail off, and the reality of how close he came to drowning hits us all hard. He blinks back tears, and I scramble for lighter thoughts.

"What? No comments about all my gear?"

He sniffs, takes a huge bite of the meat, then says, "Awesome job with all your gear, Isaiah."

"Now that's more like it." I elbow him, and he

grimaces. He's already got bruises on his arms and legs from smashing into rocks in the river.

"Boy, whoever was here last sure was messy," Sadie says.

She's right. Wrappers for caramel creams candy and chocolate bars litter the area.

Sadie slips out from under the survival blanket and starts picking up the trash, stuffing it into her pocket. *I'm just glad Ethan is now holding himself up without my help.*

Sadie freezes, staring hard at the ground.

"What is it?" I whisper, thinking snake.

She points. "This boot print is awfully familiar."

I stride over to her, my muscles feeling empty. Sure enough, I spot the clear boot print with the tread of the outside heel worn off.

"You figure these prints belong to Julie's dad?" Sadie asks.

"No way! He didn't see the break in the fence until after you took the cast of the boot print. Plus, Julie's dad was in a rush to get his cattle off park land. Besides, he got off his horse when he said hello to us, remember? I looked at his boot prints; they were slick on the bottom with a heel that was very distinct. Cowboy boots, you know? Not like these…these are more like a thick hiking boot."

"So, was the wolf hunting the cattle, and that made them go through the fence, or did a man cut the fence and try to steal the cows?"

I cross my arms, everything inside revolting against it's being the wolf's fault. "We need to see what barbed wire looks like if it has been broken by cows pushing through it. And then check the fence at the corner again."

"What's that?" Ethan points to the far side of the small clearing. There's an unusually bright green layer spread over the reddish dirt.

"It's hay," I answer, kneeling next to the thin covering, gathering up a finger full and sniffing its fresh, clean scent.

"Why is it in that weird shape?" Sadie has her hands on her hips again as she studies the crisp rectangle of cleared area, surrounded by the smattering of hay.

"I have no idea. But listen, it's been well over an hour, and Mom will be worried. Ethan, do you think you're up to walking?"

He shrugs, hugging the crinkling blanket tighter. I notice the blue tinge around his mouth has faded. "Yeah, I'm much better, thanks to you both. Maybe I'll just stay in the blanket though; my shirt feels like I'm wearing an ice cube."

I take up his sodden shirt, grateful for its cooling effect on my burning palms. I kick dirt over what's left of the fire to put it out, and we follow the trail forward, veering right.

Eventually, we stumble out onto a road.

"Hey, I think this is the road to the campground."

Ethan glances both ways, looking like a giant silver caterpillar in the blanket. "We're a lot farther away than I thought we'd be though."

"Listen." I hold up my hand for silence.

-13-

The steady hum of an engine echoes off the sharp outlines of the Teton Mountains.

"Mom says never trust a stranger." Sadie wrings her hands, peering nervously down the road.

I look at Ethan, weighing the risks. *He needs to get dry and fast. For all we know, we could be miles from the campground.*

I pull out my set of miniature binoculars from the string around my neck. "It's...a white truck." As I adjust the center knob on the binoculars, the image in the distance grows sharper. "And it's got a green stripe down the side. I'm pretty sure it's a park ranger."

We breathe a collective sigh of relief and step to the edge of the road.

Do I stick out my thumb or just wave? Turns out, it doesn't matter what I do because Sadie is leaping wildly in place, practically doing jumping jacks, and Ethan is quite a sight in his giant silver slug impression.

The big truck slows and gravel crunches as it angles off the road. A ranger sticks his head out the window. "Are you the Rawlings kids?"

"Yes, sir," I answer.

"Whew. That was an easy rescue. Come on; I'll get you back to your site." He's got his radio to his mouth as we clamber in.

"Unit 25, I've got the three children reported missing." There's a cheer on the other end, and I realize Mom and Dad might be completely losing it. "Heading toward a Gros Ventre campground now."

Ethan shivers in the crinkly blanket in the front seat, so the ranger turns up the heat. Sadie and I edge forward on the rear seat.

"I'm Dan. I've been a ranger here for 22 years. Your parents will be thrilled to see you."

"Do you have any food?" Ethan asks, "I'm starving."

"Oh," Ranger Dan says, "Let me see." He rummages on the floorboard. "All I have is one pickle from the gas station. Sorry it's not much of a selection." He holds up a fat whole pickle in a singular plastic case.

"Ummm…" Sadie says. "Your mom said no pickles, Ethan."

Ethan takes it from the ranger. "This is a matter of life and death, Sadie; I've never been this hungry. Desperate times call for desperate measures."

The sharp scent of vinegar fills the cab as he starts to crunch. Ranger Dan pulls back onto the road.

"So, what happened to y'all?"

"The cliff gave way, and Ethan fell into the river. Sadie and I fished him out." I affectionately pat the rope coiled across my chest.

Ranger Dan whistles. "I've only seen the Gros Ventre River this high once before. You can thank your lucky stars you made it out," he says to Ethan.

Ethan takes a huge bite of the dill pickle and says, "One thing's for sure, sir. Luck didn't save me; a prayer and my two cousins saved my life."

I curl my throbbing hands carefully in my lap. I'd done what needed to be done; I had given it my all, and I've never felt so full before.

"Right. I can't disagree with you there. Well, you three will be famous for a while around here. Everyone loves a happy ending."

I stare at the trees as they flash by, searching for the piercing golden eyes of the wolf, wondering if he's to blame for the cattle stampede.

"Ranger Dan?" I ask, "do you know anything about a wolf living around here?"

He catches my eyes in the rearview mirror. "Big black one?"

I nod.

-14-

"That's Kota, the last timber wolf in the Grand Teton National Park. Two years ago, we had one of the toughest winters on record. The pack crossed the frozen Gros Ventre River onto ranch land and started taking calves. Those wolves were simply doing what they had to do to survive. But by then, the ranchers had had enough. Eight wolves were shot on private land. We couldn't do anything about their slaughter." He shrugs, the sorrow still fresh on his face.

"Only Kota, the oldest male, remained. He crossed back onto park land, and now it's like he knows this place is a safe haven. So far as I know, he's never set foot out of the park again. All the experts said returning here was a death sentence for him just the same. A lone wolf could never survive the winters, not without his pack to help bring down big game. Everyone said he wouldn't survive even another season.

"What they said didn't make any difference to Kota, though. He didn't pay any attention to the statistics or the odds. He just went on living." The reverence in Ranger Dan's voice fills me too. I knew something was very special about that big black wolf; I could see the intelligence in his eyes.

"Kota." As I whisper the name, goosebumps race across my skin.

"Oh, man!" Ranger Dan hits the brakes as we round the bend in the road. Fifty cars must be lining the sides of the road, and people with cameras are leaning out through open windows. A few more courageous people are standing on the road, taking pictures of a herd of buffalo standing on the center yellow line.

"Wow!" Ethan, Sadie, and I say together. This is the closest we've seen buffalo yet.

"Wow is right. This jam could last for hours. I've got to get you to your parents straightaway. Are y'all up for a little four wheeling?"

"Yeah!" I can't contain a grin as Ranger Dan eases the truck off the road and pushes the four-wheel-drive button. The truck bumps down a slope and squeezes between two trees. "There's a trail just up ahead that will pop us out on Mormon Row Road. Have you all seen the barns there yet?"

"No," Ethan says, gripping the dash as the truck rocks back and forth. "This is awesome!"

Ranger Dan eases the truck into a small creek. We all press our noses to the windows, watching the water swirl around the tires. The truck fishtails as it struggles up the far bank.

"I think I know which cliff you fell from. It's real steep and bare, right?"

Ethan nods, shivering at the memory, finishing the pickle.

"You know, if Kota's pack was still here, you wouldn't have fallen in."

"What?" Ethan's nose wrinkles up in question, and I lean forward to hear Ranger Dan's explanation.

"It's true. The wolves determine the course of the river. Before we reintroduced wolves to the Grand Tetons in the 1990s, the riverbanks were eroding so badly that the Gros Ventre River and the Snake River would flood and change their course every year. The constantly changing river channels were a mess as massive amounts of soil and rock washed away year after year—gone forever.

"When we brought in the first of the wolves to the park, a strange phenomenon happened that year. The rivers barely changed course at all. Nobody could figure why since we had a similar rainfall to the previous year. Two years later, I was looking at satellite photos of the park in the last five years, and the light bulb went on.

"Since the wolves were released, the riverbanks

had nearly three times as much vegetation on them. Plant growth holds the soil and rocks together, which helps keep the rivers on course. But really, it was the wolves that made it happen."

"But what do wolves and plants have to do with each other since wolves only eat meat?" Sadie asks.

"The wolves frequently hunt along the riverbanks, and their constant threat forces the elk, deer, and even the buffalo to drop in for a drink and then head back to higher ground to avoid the pack. Without a thriving wolf pack, the deer eat the vegetation along the river, stripping the banks; and without the stabilizing plants, the flowing water washed away the soil.

"So, really, the wolves are responsible for keeping the land healthy. Everything is connected. And there you have it. Ethan, if we had had an entire wolf pack, the banks would've held, and we never would have had a reason to meet."

-15-

Ranger Dan revs the engine as we emerge from the wooded trail and onto another paved road.

"This is Mormon Row. Even though this route is the long way around, it's still faster than waiting for buffalo to finish napping."

I'm still wrapped up in Kota's story and how the wolf has withstood what should have killed him. *I bet he misses his family. I sure wish Kota could find a new family. Finding one would be a miracle.*

I think of Poppa's knife and wonder where I lost it. I feel so bad I was careless enough to misplace it. *Finding it will also take a miracle.*

"See those barns there?" Ranger Dan points

to a huge wooden barn with a peaked roof. "T.A. Moulton built it in the 1920s."

I must admit, with the sharp snowcapped mountains in the distance, the scene is breathtaking. Four or five cars are parked there, and people are taking pictures.

"These two barns are the most famous, but other historic barns are in the park. One is fairly close to where I picked you up. But that one is in bad shape, and there's no road to it. Not many folks know it's even there."

Soon we're nearly back to the campground, but Kota is still heavy on my mind. I'm more determined than ever to prove that he wasn't to blame for the stampede. The four-wheeler tracks that Sadie had cast might be a helpful lead.

"Ranger Dan? Are four-wheelers allowed in the park?"

"No, sir. Permits for ATVs are only for park rangers or law enforcement officials."

"So there might be some tracks in the park from

rangers riding them?" I frown at what seems like a dead-end lead.

Ranger Dan seems uncertain. "I don't recall any of our rangers using an ATV this season; and now that y'all aren't lost anymore, we won't have any law enforcement riding around either." He smiles as he turns into the campground and takes a left around the loop. Hope fills my heart again. *Maybe the ATV tracks are what we're looking for.*

Mom is standing at our tent with her hands over her mouth, tears running down her face, and Dad has his arm around her shoulders. They practically crush us with hugs as we get out of the truck. Mom can't stop touching us, patting our heads, rubbing our backs, searching our faces.

"Mom. We're fine. Really," I declare.

She sniffs, nodding, not believing me at all. "Are you hungry? I bet you are. I'll stoke the fire, and we can make more stick bread. It was fast and delicious too."

Soon enough we were nibbling soft, steaming

bread from our roasting sticks. Ethan is like a bottomless pit, and I think he's eaten ten pounds of bread by the time he stops.

I scan the distance with the Tetons hedging everything in. Sure wish I could see Kota again—the lone survivor who had defied all odds and created a different outcome than anyone could've believed. *I've just got to prove his innocence.*

"Mom, do you want to take a walk with me? I want to look at the fence again real quick."

"Of course, honey. Anyone else want to come?"

Ethan had eaten too much and wouldn't be moving for a while. Sadie was busy making designs in the red sand with pebbles and sticks.

"I'll stay here with these two," Dad says, while sitting with his arms behind his head, happier than I've ever seen him.

As we hike, Mom chatters nonstop. I can tell it will be a while until her relief of having us back wears off. "Look how pretty the river is."

"Well, I've seen enough of it for now."

She grabs my arm, looking relieved. "I guess so."

We reach the fence, and I squat down, studying the repair job the cowboys had done. They twisted a short loop into the thick wire on the left. Then they put the long end through and wound the longer strand back around itself to make it tight again.

"Mom, does it seem to you that if a bunch of cattle had pushed through here, each wire would've broken at a random place?"

"Hmmm," she says, bending down. "It does look rather clean, doesn't it? Almost like the wires were cut."

"That's what I think too." I stand, gingerly dusting off my hands. Behind the shelter of the corner post, I see a patch of light-green vegetation with small orange and red flowers. "Hang on," I mutter, flipping through my survival guide. *Jewel weed. Good for burns, rashes, and most skin conditions; also edible.* I pull up a handful and crush it into my palms. The juice is cool against the rope burn, and almost instantly my hand feels better.

"We better hurry back," I say as I stand.

"Why?"

I lick a finger and hold it up to the wind. "Because I do believe those black clouds are coming our way."

She looks up at the peaks where an ominous bank of clouds sits over the mountains like a giant fur coat.

"Oh," she says.

Still, by the time we crawl into our sleeping bags that night, the clouds remain hunched over the distant mountains.

-16-

Something is ripping at our tent. I wake up, shouting at the sudden movement. The repaired poles barely hold as the tent flexes hard.

"It's a T-Rex!" Ethan shouts in the pitch dark.

Thunder vibrates the ground under us, and seconds later lightning illuminates the interior of our tent.

If I look half as terrified as Ethan does, we're in sad shape. I scramble to my feet and fumble for my flashlight.

"Boys!" Dad's shout jolts me out of the tent.

"Everything's blowing away! Grab what you can and then get in the truck." He snatches at a folding chair as it cartwheels away. The first fat drops of icy rain pelt against my neck.

"Sadie!" I shout, as the sky lets loose, soaking us to the skin instantly. The crazed wind snatches at my words. "Get Mom's bed off the tent floor!"

She turns from chasing another chair and fumbles in the rain, the zipper resisting her attempts.

"Here! Let me help!" I force the zipper open, and we step inside shedding pools of water. "Get it up off the ground, or we may never camp again!" We struggle with the thick pad Mom and Dad have been sleeping on. "Roll it up and tilt it against the corner."

We pile Sadie's sleeping bag on top as the wind sucks hard at the thin fabric of the tent.

"Let's get your stuff," Sadie shouts over the roar of the wind.

We step out into the chaos of the storm. The raindrops are so big it's like being under a faucet. Mom is rushing after the plastic bin she keeps our utensils in as it skitters toward the road.

Ethan emerges from our tent "I got our stuff…."
A massive crack of thunder drowns out his next
words.

Sadie plows into my side, wrapping me in a terrified bear hug.

"Get in the truck now!" Dad commands as the
lightning blinds us momentarily. We scramble
in, our clothes sticking, making it hard to move.
Ethan is the last one to shut his door, blocking out
the storm. We sit, panting hard, soaking the seats.

Mom turns in slow motion toward us in the back-
seat, water streaming down her face. She makes a
strange sound, puts a hand over her mouth, then
breaks into all-out laughter. Next thing I know,
we're in fits of giggling that are nearly impossible
to stop.

Finally, Mom manages to say, "The good news
is that all our dry clothes are in a watertight bin in
the back of the truck."

"How about breakfast at the Jenny Lake Lodge?
They should be open in an hour," Dad says.

"Well, I'm not cooking over a *water pit*, that's for sure," Mom says.

The rain pounds for the entire 45 minutes it takes us to drive to the lodge.

"I bet the river will be really high now," I comment.

"I've been soaked twice already in the last 24 hours, and I don't even want to think about that river," Ethan says.

Having breakfast at the lodge after getting into dry clothes is like a taste of heaven. I believe I could probably eat two full breakfast plates. I stuff some crispy hash browns into my mouth with my fingers.

"Did you know we were supposed to be hit by a storm?" Sadie asks.

Dad answers, "Well, I guess I must have missed that weather broadcast, Sadie." Dad chuckles.

"Maybe this happened for a reason…so I can have something that really fills me up! I'm not used to eating so light."

Mom nods enthusiastically. "Definitely! Part of that includes using your fork."

My hand hangs in midair, with a bunch of hash browns dangling from my fingers. "Sure, Mom."

I drop the food on my plate and pick up my fork. Dad keeps eyeing Mom, and I can tell what he's thinking. *This is the end of camping as a family. We have surely pushed Mom past her limits now.*

"Maybe we're not cut out for camping," he ventures.

-17-

Ethan, Sadie, and I freeze, holding our breath while we all stare at Mom.

She is cradling a steaming cup of coffee, her brown eyes studying each of us before answering, "I don't know about that."

She arches a brow at Dad. "The kids saved our bed. That gesture was certainly selfless and thoughtful. Besides, we're always telling them not to quit."

I sigh dramatically, "Yeah, it's tough being a kid when you're always saving your mom."

Sadie grabs my arm in excitement under the table as Mom continues. "Kids, what do you think?

Now that you've had a mouthful of camping, how does it taste?"

"I love it!" Sadie can't contain the words.

I try for every button I can push with my answer. "Well, Mom, I've learned a lot about the park, survival, and I think *next time* we could do it even better."

"Air mattresses would be absolutely lovely." Mom nods behind her coffee. "What about you, Ethan?"

"Well, Aunt Ruth, I appreciate you bringing me." He looks at Sadie and me. "And I sure am glad my cousins were with me yesterday. If I promise to stay away from cliffs, can I come along next time too?"

She looks out the window. "I've always wanted to see the Great Smoky Mountains."

"Yes!" we three kids shout, then hunker down on the bench as the whole restaurant turns to look at us. Dad's grin is wider than I've ever seen it as he wraps one arm around Mom and then kisses the top of her head.

We pile back into the truck after spreading towels on the soaked seats. I stare out the window, calling out each creature that I see. "Three elk! Oh, there's a herd of bighorn sheep!" They graze on the steep hillside, dotted by silvery sagebrush.

We cross the bridge over the Snake River near the area named Moose, and Sadie says, "Look at the river! It's twice as deep as when we went to breakfast!"

"Five buffalo," I call, pointing at the riverbank.

"Don't fall in!" Ethan calls down to the animals.

"Three moose!" They're the first moose we've seen, and Dad slows down so we can see them.

Then we're on the long barren stretch called Antelope Flats Road. By the time Dad turns onto Mormon Row Road, Ethan is grimacing. A weird gurgling noise is coming from his stomach!

He groans, leaning forward. "Ummm...Uncle Greg? Oh...I... Could you pull over? *Fast!*"

-18-

"For what, Ethan?" Dad asks, not slowing down a bit.

"I might... Oh... *Pull over!*" He shouts the last bit, his face now desperate.

Dad nearly locks up the brakes, pulling off the road near Ditch Creek, where Ranger Dan had taken us four-wheeling. Ethan jumps from the truck before it comes to a complete halt.

"Pickles..." he groans before his feet hit the ground, running for the thick cover near the creek.

Mom watches him sprint until he disappears into the brush. "Did he happen to eat a pickle?"

"Yep," Sadie whispers.

"When?" Mom asks.

"Well, it was the only food in Ranger Dan's truck," I answer.

Mom quickly covers her mouth with her hand, not quite concealing her smile. "His mom said pickles give him gastrointestinal issues. Oh, dear. Poor Ethan."

"He said desperate times call for different desperate measures," I say, eyeing a big one-ton truck that slows down next to us.

Dad rolls down his window as the other driver does the same.

"That's Julie's dad!" Sadie says, scooting to Ethan's side of the truck and rolling down the window.

"Are you all right?" Julie's dad asks with a tip of his hat.

"Yes, thank you. One of the kids needed…a pit-stop," Dad answers.

Sadie leans out the window, waving. "How's Julie?"

The man frowns. "Not doing too good, I'm

afraid. All three of her competition horses were stolen last night."

Sadie sucks in a horrified breath. "Oh, no!"

He nods. "Right before the final rodeo of the year too. Y'all didn't have any horses stampeding over your tent, did you?"

"No," Dad answers, "just one big storm."

"Yeah, that's the same one that obliterated all the tracks of the thieves." He hits the steering wheel with his palm.

"I was hoping maybe they were loose on park land, but I haven't had any luck here. Tell you what, take my number, will you? If you see anything that could point us in the right direction, please let me know."

Dad adds his number to his phone directory, and Julie's dad drives off.

"Honey," Mom lays her hand on Dad's arm. "You're going to need to take this to Ethan." She holds out a paper towel. Dad frowns at her, but she doesn't back off.

"Right." He takes the towel and hops out of the truck.

Sadie turns to me with tears in her eyes. "We've got to help Julie! She must be so worried. Poor Timber."

I shake my head, my mind racing. "The cattle stampede must be connected somehow. What do we know about it? The fence seems to have been cut—not knocked down by stampeding cows. There were boot tracks and four-wheeler tracks, # 10 nails, and wolf prints." I chew on my bottom lip, wishing something new would surface in my mind.

"Don't forget that bit of red fabric that was stuck to the fence," Sadie adds.

I snap my fingers. "Yeah, right. Then we found the exact boot print at the camp near the river."

Sadie nods. "…with lots of caramel candy wrappers."

"So, it's possible Julie's dad is right, and the horses have been hidden in the park somewhere."

Dad and Ethan emerge from the woods, and we recount the awful news to Ethan. He smashes his fist into his palm, stomach forgotten. "I can't believe it!"

-19-

By the time we reach site A-68, I can almost
see the smoke rising from Ethan's brain. We talk
about possibilities for all the clues, but two things
continue to throw me for a loop. *Why were there
wolf tracks near the stampede? What was Kota doing there? That wolf knows more than anyone else
about this mystery, that's for sure. Second, did the
same man who tried to steal the cows take Julie's
horses? We should have asked her dad if any cows
were taken too.*

I chew on these ideas while we rebuild our camp
after the storm. The chairs have blown all the way
down to the second campground loop, and my re-

paired tent poles have given out under the harsh hand of the wind, leaving a large cold puddle on the left side of our tent floor.

Ethan and I are still struggling with it when he says, "Am I hearing things, or are hoofbeats coming this way again?" I look around our tent site that seems to have grown wet fabric. Mom was hanging our wet towels and clothes everywhere she could—even on the tree branches.

Sadie cocks her head, holding perfectly still over the pool that is our firepit. "No, I can hear them too."

She jams the stick she's been digging with at the base of the metal ring one more time, and the ash-filled water lets loose, running straight for our tent.

"Sadie!" I try to redirect the dirty water with my boot, but the firepit is draining hard now, and there's no stopping the flow.

"Sorry! Dad told me to do it."

I groan. At least the dirty water washes into the

corner that's already wet. Ethan suddenly abandons our repair job and rushes to the edge of the campsite, shielding his eyes with his hand as he looks at the approaching rider. "It's Julie!"

His voice cracks when he says her name, and I chuckle as Sadie and I join him. Julie rides up on a brown horse. I notice her shoulders are slumped when she reaches us. She starts to say something, then bites her lip, and instead, brushes a tear from her eye.

"Have you found out anything about your horses yet?" Sadie asks.

"No. They're just…gone, and now I can't win High Point this year either, and…" Her face looks pained as she forces out her words. "I just wish I knew they were safe! That they had feed. I've spent the last two years with them every day. They're… well, I know it sounds stupid, but they're my best friends."

I touch the soft nose of the horse she's riding. "Couldn't you ride this one at the rodeo?"

"No. I mean, he's a great ranch horse, but he has no training for competition. That kind of preparation takes years."

"The *houses*...I mean, horses might turn up." A blush creeps up Ethan's neck as he continues. "A lot can happen in two too...ugh, two days."

I feel bad for my cousin, tripping over his words like that, so I jump in. "Are horses allowed in the park?"

She nods, "Yeah, people can bring them in to ride on certain trails, and horseback riding tours are offered throughout the park or there's me, hoping to find any sign of my boys."

"It would've been easier if there weren't other horses in the Tetons. Were they out in the pasture when they went missing?"

Julie slides off her mount. "No, I've been riding them every day to tune them up for the rodeo, so they were in stalls overnight."

"Were any other *hoses*..." Ethan stammers, "I mean horses...stolen or just yours?"

"Just mine. Timber, Junior, and Flash."

"Timber is a Palomino. What do the other two look like?" Sadie asks.

"Junior is a black-and-white paint with bright blue eyes. And Flash is a bay with three white socks, or legs."

"Were there any tracks?" I ask.

"No, the rain made sure of that."

"Oh, right."

Ethan snaps his fingers. "Can you think of anyone who would want to steal them?"

Wow! He's improving! He didn't say seal instead of steal.

"Well, Cindy and I have been competing for High Point all year, but we get along pretty good; and the girl who came in third this year lives on the northeast corner of Wyoming, so she generally doesn't even ride in the same shows we do."

"What about a boyfriend? Did you dump a guy recently?" Ethan's voice seems a little strained as he asks these questions.

Julie puts a hand on her hip, looks him straight in the eye, and says, "Nope."

"Nope what? You don't have a boyfriend, or you haven't dumped one?"

Julie turns to the horse, tightening the girth around his belly. "Don't have one. Too busy riding and helping Daddy on the ranch." A hint of a smile shows on Ethan's mouth as Julie swings easily into the saddle.

"Well," she sighs, "I better get back to the ranch." Her shoulders droop again. "Maybe I'll sit in the bleachers and watch the rodeo with y'all."

"No!" Ethan declares so forcefully she turns in her saddle to look at him as he adds, "You'll be riding. Anything could happen in two days. You'll see."

She smiles at him. "Thanks, Ethan. I hope you're right."

Julie spurs the horse, and we follow her to the top of the hill, watching as she veers right after she reaches the ranch fence and fades into the distance.

As we turn to head back, we notice a cloud of dust rising on the plain in the opposite direction.

"What's that?" Sadie asks.

-20-

I pull out my binoculars to study the area underneath the cloud. "Buffalo, I think."

A few minutes later, the herd is close enough to see with the naked eye.

"Dad!" Sadie shouts, making me plug my ears. "Can we hike down to see the buffaloes?"

"Bison," I correct her.

Dad strides up the hill, shadowing his eyes as he looks over the plain. "Sure, honey. That creek will be between us, so we won't be too close." He waves to Mom, and we set off toward the now-familiar far corner of the fence.

Dad, Ethan and Sadie creep down toward the

creek, counting the huge creatures that are now grazing among the sage.

"Dad, I'm going to stay near the fence, and I'll catch up in a minute," I whisper.

He surveys the area, then nods.

Something has got to give in this strange case of stampeding cows and missing horses. I reach the corner and squat down in front of the repair in the fence, determined to figure out what's been bothering me so much about it.

I gasp. *Weren't the long-twisted ends of the repair facing to the right when Mom and I were here? And weren't the short loops toward the left?* By the time we get back to the campsite, I can't hold back the question.

Mom wrinkles her nose, looking up to one side. "I'm sorry, I don't remember. But listen, everybody, another camper just told me that the park has something called the Junior Ranger program. You can get a booklet at the visitor center. After you've completed the required activities for your age, a ranger signs it and initiates you. Do you want to earn some badges?"

What I'm really hoping for is to find some clues that will point us toward Julie's horses. Hanging around the campsite isn't going to get that done.

"I could be a *real* park ranger?" Sadie's eyes light up at the possibility.

Mom shrugs, smiling. "A junior one, yes."

"Go!" Sadie shouts.

"I guess we've come to a decision," Dad says.

We all load into the truck for the long ride back to the Jenny Lake Visitor Center.

———

The ranger hands Ethan, Sadie and me colorful booklets, and I flip through the pages. *Wait!* Desperately, I flip backward. *What was that?* On page 8, it says "Restore History" at the top of the booklet. I scan the page, eyes wide. The text says we are supposed to visit three historic cabins in the park, and then finish the drawings on the page.

Something Ranger Dan had said earlier comes

back in a rush. *"There are other old structures in the park, but they're in bad shape."* I finger the nail in my pocket with that funny feeling tickling in my chest again.

"Ethan, Sadie, look at this!" I tap page eight with the nail. Ethan's mouth falls open, snatching the nail from my hand. "Do you think…the horses are possibly hidden in a historic building in the park?" He flips over the nail, studying it as if it's a long-lost key. "If you were planning on stealing horses and hiding them here in the park, you would have to do some repairs to those old buildings in bad shape to keep them in, right?"

We nod in unison.

-21-

"So, what activity do you want to do first?" Mom asks.

"Page eight!" Ethan says, his eyes bright. "Can we visit one of these historic sites, Aunt Ruth?"

Mom smiles. "Of course. That's a great idea." She asks Dad to get directions to the closest site.

"Before we leave, let's use the restrooms first."

Ethan heads into a bathroom stall. His stomach is still making a few loud noises, and I feel like I could do the same. I sit thinking with my chin resting on my palm. As I try to put all the pieces together, my brain churns for the missing links.

The one aspect that consistently doesn't fit is

Kota. *What was he doing off park land when Ranger Dan said he hadn't gone beyond the park borders for two years?*

I hear the shuffle of boots as someone else enters the restroom…and then voices.

"…worked like a charm."

Then I hear a snort of laughter from a different voice that says, "Till you nearly ruined it all…"

Their rough laughter makes my stomach tighten. *Those voices sound like the same group we saw at the store.*

I lean to the side, peering through the crack in the stall door. A figure with a red-checkered flannel coat is washing his hands. My skin starts to crawl. His voice makes me shudder because it sounds so much like Max Smith's. I swallow hard as he continues.

"She'll be sure to go out with you now after all this…and you facing down a wolf for her." I see another teen elbow him as they pass by the crack between the door and the frame. I freeze as I watch each pair of boots shuffle past. I sure wish they could leave a print on this hard floor! I hear the main doors swish close.

I rush out of the bathroom, searching for the group, but they're not in the visitors' center any more. I slam a fist into my palm, then wince in pain. The burns don't hurt unless I do something like that. *Wait!* I rush toward the doors and pick up a caramel cream candy wrapper.

Sadie walks over, her face as shocked as mine.

"Did you see who dropped this?" I ask.

Ethan comes toward us, tucking in his shirt. As he walks up, he leans over to whisper, "Isaiah, did you hear them talking about a wolf?"

I nod.

"Let's head over to the old ferry," Dad interrupts.

Mom looks through Sadie's Junior Ranger booklet when we're in the truck. "Oh, look at this. The program is arranged by age groups. Each group is required to complete a different number of activities. Ages seven and under are in the wolf group. Then ages eight through ten…Sadie, that's you, and you're a bear. You must choose at least five activities to complete. Then Isaiah and Ethan, you're in the bison group, and you must choose at least seven activities. Also, every activity marked with an arrow must be completed by all ages."

I focus on page 2 of my booklet, trying to push off the failure of not getting out of the restroom more quickly. I see a silhouette of a moose named Murie that is hidden on 12 different pages of the booklet. I start to hunt for him until we pull up at the historic Menors Ferry General Store parking area.

The hike to get to both the ferry and the store are short, paved, and flat. Dad, Ethan, and I are drawn in by the ferry with its old wooden pontoons that point upriver, as well as the on/off ramp for the horses and wagons that sits on top.

The cable system used to draw the ferry across the Snake River is sunk deep into the earth on each bank. *I imagine myself spurring my horse, hearing his hooves strike the echoing wood of the ferry, hoping the whole way across that he doesn't spook and plunge us both into the cold river.*

"Come on, guys! Let's go see the general store." I jump at Sadie's voice as she pulls me out of my imagination.

The general store has tons of historical stuff, like the scythe used to cut hay. The first thing I notice is the lack of plastic; everything is glass, metal or wood.

Mom sucks in a long breath through her nose. "I sure hope they still sell the cookies that I'm smelling."

We get in line, and soon I'm holding a hot, gooey chocolate chip cookie in my hands.

Sadie frowns at Mom. "Do I get my own cookie?" Her brown eyes are huge; and I'm glad I'm not the one telling her no because I would probably cave in so we wouldn't have to deal with Sadie the tornado.

"Honey, you and I are going to share," Mom

says. Admittedly, Mom only gives Sadie a third of the cookie, which she stuffs into her mouth all at once.

"UGH! It is so GOOD!" Sadie shivers with delight.

Mom and I look at each other, horrified. *One third was too much!*

"WAHHHOOO! THIS PLACE IS INCREDIBLE!" Sadie shouts, spinning in circles.

"Oh, dear," Mom says, right before Sadie takes off down the path. "Greg! You've got to keep up with her! And don't let her near the river!"

-22-

Dad takes off in yet another impressive sprint.

"What's going on?" Ethan questions, licking gooey chocolate off his fingers.

"Haven't you noticed the suspicious lack of s'mores around a campfire? Or any sugar, for that matter?"

"Yeah, I keep wondering when Aunt Ruth is going to break them out."

"Well, she's not going to—no way. Have you ever made one of those volcanoes with baking soda and vinegar in school? Well, the result is the perfect picture of Sadie and sugar mixed together." I make a fizzing sound and mime an explosion with my hands.

"Oh," Ethan says, but I can tell he doesn't really get the big picture.

"Let's put it this way, Ethan: I'd rather live a sugarless life then have to deal with her when she eats some."

"Come on," Mom orders. "We better try to find them; they could be halfway back to Kentucky by now."

We pass an open-style barn full of old wooden carriages and wagons at a fast clip and finally come upon Dad and Sadie back near the ferry. Sadie is swinging like an orangutan from the ferry cable.

"Get off there, Sadie!" Dad bellows from far below her on the ground.

"OKAY!" she shouts, letting go at the apex of her swing and soaring through the air. She lands like she's an Olympic gymnast, her hands high in the air, perfectly balanced. Then she takes off giggling, wild-eyed, hands waving above her head.

"Sadie!" Dad's voice has a tinge of desperation in it.

I catch a flitting glimpse of her as she darts through a small group of trees.

"Catch her!" Mom shouts, running forward. Ethan and I jog after them.

"How bad can it be?" Ethan asks, still in the dark.

"Well," I puff, "I think the sugar shuts down her logical brain, and she becomes a wild animal...." I haul in a breath, "for at least 15 minutes."

"There!" Ethan points to the left, and I catch a streak of motion in the woods as well. We veer off the trail, cutting around sagebrush.

"Watch for snakes!" I yell as we start to climb the foot of a hill. The trees thicken, separating Ethan and me as we climb.

Ahead, I catch movement from the corner of my eye.

"Sadie!" I groan, breathing too hard now to shout. *Why does she have to lead us on this wild goose chase?*

I lean forward, using my hands to help me climb the reddish shale up to a wide ledge. As I scan the

———

pine trees scattered around, the scent of them is strong in my lungs, but I still don't see any movement. As my breathing slows, I hear the scrape of one rock against another.

-23-

Stepping in that general direction, I wonder if I will rejoin Ethan up ahead. The stinging bite of pine needles makes me throw up my arms to protect my face as I twist through the dense evergreens.

The branches fall away as I press forward, but before I lower my arms, that feeling strikes in my chest. My hair stands on end. I freeze, listening hard, but the mountainside is dead quiet. *Too quiet.* Slowly, I drop my arms, heart pounding. Not ten yards ahead, Kota is sitting still watching me, his wide head nearly as tall as my chin.

Our eyes lock, golden on bright blue. Primal

fear echoes in my mind, and yet within those wise eyes, I don't find any savage intent.

"Kota," I whisper reverently, struck by the size of his paws. They were designed that way to keep the wolf from sinking deep in the heavy winter snow. His muscles ripple under his long, coarse fur as his nose twitches, searching the air.

Kota the survivor. Faced with odds stacked high against him, he simply kept going. I put a hand slowly to my chest, absorbing his strength.

He licks his lips, leaps and turns in a flash, fading into the trees. *How does an animal of that size disappear so quickly?* I rush forward, desperate to see him again. He's standing just ahead, watching me over his shoulder. When he sees me, he sets off at a steady trot.

"You want me to follow you?" I whisper, unable to do anything else. I trot forward, following him up the next incline as I catch frequent glimpses of him here and there.

Finally, I scramble onto a flat, huge rock slab.

Directly ahead of me I see the small, dark mouth of a cave. Scattered everywhere on the slab are an odd assortment of items: a glove, a wallet, an empty camera bag. *Has Kota eaten all the people these things belong to?* I shiver at the thought.

Struggling to slow my wild breathing from the climb, I can't keep myself from pushing forward, wondering how big his cave is.

A deep reverberating growl echoes out of the cave, making me jump into the air and scramble backward to the far edge of the rock slab, crouched, ready to run.

"Okay, so I'm not allowed in your house. That's fair enough," I mutter.

Kota reappears, stepping from the mouth of the cave, the king of the forest. He advances slowly until only scant feet separate us, and I'm trembling. Every instinct is screaming at me to run. Yet I'm mesmerized by his soul-piercing gaze.

He lowers his head, and I hear metal striking against rock. In a flash he returns to the mouth of the cave to sit with his bushy tail wrapped over his front paws.

I breathe deeply to calm my beating heart, finally lowering my eyes to the place he had stopped, and I had heard the sound. *Poppa's knife!* A glimmer of light filtering through the trees shows it's still wet from being in his mouth.

"You found this? Out by Jenny Lake?" I ask Kota. His nose twitches in response. I look around at the scattering of items. "You collect the things you find in the park, don't you? I bet it helps you feel less lonely."

As I slowly reach for Papa's knife, I can see myself at school, facing Max Smith. I am Kota, and Max is my cruel winter. My hand closes on the knife. Just like Kota, against all odds, I will overcome the "winter." I grip the knife tight, sealing in my resolve. I won't listen to Max anymore— just like Kota wouldn't listen to those who said he couldn't survive alone. *I'll make sure my thick "wolf fur" keeps out his ice-cold words.*

Just beyond where the knife lay, I see a dark patch of dirt with a clear set of Kota's fresh prints. I scowl at them, noticing his right front print has a deep gash through the main pad. *It must be an old scar.* And his left front print shows a smaller outside toe than the others. Everyone had commented on how perfect Sadie's plaster cast of the print was. Kota's are far from perfect, scarred by his determination to survive.

I lock eyes with him again. "It wasn't you at the stampede, was it? You don't leave park land anymore. Right, boy?"

Elation fills me, knowing that Kota hadn't been involved. I clutch the knife tightly in my palm. Really, Kota has given me so much more than just a keepsake. I now have the determination to survive my winter too.

"Thank you, Kota," I whisper, heart in my throat. A twig snaps down the hill, making me glance that way. When I look back, Kota is gone.

"Isaiah!" Ethan shouts.

I turn, dropping down the slope, needing to keep Kota's lair hidden.

"Did you find her?" he asks when we meet far below.

"Find who?"

He rolls his eyes. "Your sister, of course."

"No. But I found this." I reverently hold out the pocketknife. It's still damp.

Ethan makes a face. "How did it get way up here? You lost it near Jenny Lake, and this is the first time we've ever hiked anywhere near Moose."

I open my mouth, then close it quickly, unable to tell him about Kota. Our meeting just seems too sacred.

Dad's shout ripples up the hill and saves me from answering. "Boys, come on, we've got Sadie. Let's finish page 8."

-24-

As I lie in my sleeping bag with my icy-cold nose, every joint sore from being pressed against the hard ground all night, and dampness seeping in, I can't help but think, *It's awesome! I love every part of camping, uncomfortable or not.* The sharp scent of wood smoke fills my nostrils as the first pale fingers of dawn reach through the tent fabric.

I struggle out of my bag, and I manage to present Mom with another cup of hot coffee as she steps out of the tent. Watching the sun come up over the mountains with her is perfect. "Mom, this has been the greatest week of my whole life."

"Really? I'm so glad you enjoyed it! It's hard to

believe we've only more two days and two nights left in this incredible place."

I hug her tight, and when Sadie wakes up and steps out, we absorb her into our hug and watch the mist burn off the plains in the warm sun.

"Can we finish earning our ranger badges today, Mom?" Sadie asks.

"Ummm, we better. Tomorrow is our last day, and we'll be at the rodeo for most of that."

I frown. "Seeing Julie there without her horses will be hard, though. I've just got this feeling…"

"The same kind of feeling you had last summer before I stepped on that nail?" Mom asks.

"Yeah, that one."

"Well, what exactly is that *feeling* telling you? I'm a believer in the feeling since I didn't listen to it the first time, and I should have."

I shrug. "It says that I should know where those horses are. They're closer than we think."

"If you get any solid ideas, I'm up for checking them out." Mom's vote of confidence makes me smile. "Come on. We're down to crackers and cheese for breakfast, so let's eat and then head out to the Jenny Lake Visitor Center to finish up those activity books."

When we get in the truck, I check off the pages I've already completed:

☑ Play Ranger bingo.

☑ Keep a clean camp.

☑ Hike the Tetons.

☑ Restore history.

☑ Follow the fire.

☑ Sculpt to the range.

☑ Explore habitats.

☑ Imagine the future.

☑ Map it.

☑ Do the "Prepare-for-Winter" maze.

(Though the activity was below my age group, it looked really fun, and it was!)

I work on page 17, "Match and Adapt" while

Dad drives. At the bottom I'm supposed to draw an imaginary animal that has adaptations to be better suited for its environment. I draw a horse with wings because it seems like that was what Timber grew.

"Ethan, did you do page 17?" I ask.

He flips through his book. "Yep."

"Let me see it." I take his book and study what he drew and finally ask, "What is it?"

"It's a velociraptor with fur to survive the cold, and heat-sensing pits like a viper to find prey in the deep woods, and webbed feet so it can stay on top of deep snow."

"Wow!" I say because I can't think of anything else. I hand the book back to him.

"So, what else do you all need to do to become junior rangers?" Dad asks.

"I need to attend a ranger-led activity; everything else is done." I answer.

"Me too," Ethan adds.

"Me three," adds Sadie, and I am so glad to have

her non-sugared self, sitting next to me in the truck today.

"Great. I saw a schedule posted for ranger-led events at the visitor's center." Dad turns into the parking lot, and I scan the water of Jenny Lake.

"Moose!" I say, pressing my nose against the glass, watching water run from the huge bull moose's antlers as he lifts his head.

"Two *meese!*" Sadie exclaims.

"Two moose," Mom corrects.

"Right!"

"I only found Murie the moose on nine pages; maybe the ranger will count this sighting as numbers 10 and 11," I say, referring to the book as my breath fogs the window.

The only ranger-led activity this morning is a demonstration on making an arrowhead from stone. Ranger Dan leads it, and we're the only ones there, so he lets us come up and chip the flint stones ourselves as he spreads them on the table.

"Take a scrap of deer hide to protect your hand

as you hold the piece of flint; then use one of the dense river rocks to chip away at the edges of your arrowhead." He shows us, but it looks way easier when he does it. Getting everything held just right so I can strike the thin edges and not crack the whole thing in half like Ethan has already done twice is much more difficult than I would have thought.

While I work at it, I argue with myself about telling Ranger Dan where Kota's cave is.

"When you've got the basic shape, then take a section of the deer antler and press it hard against the edges, flipping the flint over as you go so it gets good and sharp."

Slowly, but surely, the three of us follow Ranger Dan's instructions and work carefully.

Sadie finally holds hers up. It's as perfect as an arrow made from primitive tools can be! Mine is lopsided but is still one of the coolest things I've ever done.

Ethan holds up the two halves of his third attempt. "Maybe I'll just pay Sadie to make arrow-heads for me."

We all laugh.

"Only if you pay me in cookies," she declares.

A stark quiet descends over us as we imagine what Sadie and multiple cookies would look like.

"Oh. Maybe I'll have to be a vegetarian then."

I pat Ethan's shoulder. "That would be the better choice."

"What is that?" Sadie asks, pointing to a bright area of ground near the visitor's center.

Ranger Dan explains, "That's some straw spread over new grass seed to keep it safe while it grows. Did you know no one is allowed to bring straw or hay into a national park unless it's been tested against foreign weed seeds? They could start to grow and take over the natural plants in the area."

Ranger Dan points at the arrowheads we chipped from the flint. "How about if you take these home with you?"

"Yes!" Sadie squeals, but I'm trapped still looking at the bright area of straw with that feeling spreading across my chest with a strength I've never felt before. Regrettably, I can't place what it's trying to get me to see. I clench my jaw, gripping my arrowhead so hard it nearly cut my palm.

"Isaiah?" Ranger Dan says.

I jerk out of the sensation and realize he's been calling my name. "I've already scored and signed Sadie's and Ethan's books. Are you ready?"

"Sure, sure." I pull the rolled-up book from my back pocket and stare at the straw again, chewing my lip while he checks my work.

"Looks like you all are ready to take the Junior Ranger pledge. Raise your right hand."

We raise our hands, and Ranger Dan starts, "As a Junior Ranger…"

We repeat after him in unison, and as the words settled deep inside of me, I know that for the rest of my life I'll do my best to uphold this pledge.

I am proud to be a National Park Service Junior Ranger. I promise to appreciate, respect, and protect all national park places. I also promise to continue learning about the landscape, plants, animals and history of these special places. I will share what I learn with my friends and family.

We finish the pledge, and I can't help grinning as Ranger Dan hands out our badges with a bull moose walking in front of the Tetons.

I turn, nearly forgetting not to smile as Mom takes her picture of us holding up our arrowhead and badge.

"Wait!" I cry just as the flash goes off. All the pieces suddenly come together in my mind.

-25-

"I know where the horses are!"

I sprint for the truck as if my life depends on it. "Hurry!" I shout to my family over my shoulder.

When they finally reach the truck, I'm nearly frantic, my racing thoughts at full throttle.

"Isaiah, what is going on?" Dad asks as I bear-hug Sadie, stuff her into the truck, then climb in behind her.

"Drive toward camp, Dad, and I'll tell you on the way!"

Dad shakes his head and pulls out of the visitors' center. We're nearly to the bridge at Moose before I can untangle my thoughts enough to get them out of my mouth, and Ethan is about to lose it entirely.

"It's the straw!" I say over Sadie and Ethan's clamor, asking me to tell where the horses are. "After seeing it near the visitor center, it got stuck in my brain like it was ultra-important to this mystery. Don't you see it?"

"No!" they shout at me.

"Okay," I pull out the nail we had picked up from the stampede. "It all fits together perfectly, and if I'm right, Julie will get to compete tomorrow just like she planned!"

"ISAIAH!" Ethan's face is red, his eyes bugging.

"They never meant to steal any cows! Can't you see it? They were going in to snatch Julie's horses the night of the stampede! They cut the fence at its point closest to the park land, and then they went to nab the horses. But the whole herd of cattle was headed that way at breakneck pace because a wolf was hot on their heels."

I see it all so clearly; it's like watching a movie.

"The thieves got out of the herd's way, but then they saw a lone wolf standing there, staring them down. It wasn't Kota though; his prints are far from perfect after all he has survived." I stroke my chin, wondering about that.

"When Ethan fell into the river and we rescued him, we didn't know any horses had been stolen the night before. We were trying to find our way back, and we came to a hidden camp where we built a fire to warm you up, and we found the same boot prints! Plus, didn't it seem like a four-wheeler had smashed down the trail? Then, we saw that strange shape where the hay had been spread on the ground."

I lean back in my seat, smacking my forehead as the thought hits me. "How could I have been so dense? They had a hay bale on the back of a four-wheeler because they had to feed the stolen horses something!" I lower my voice and whisper, "I'd be willing to bet they didn't have their hay inspected for foreign weeds either!"

I hit my leg with my fist. "Remember, Ranger Dan told us that an old barn was right near where he had picked us up after the river disaster?"

Sadie has both hands on her cheeks, mouth hanging open. "You're right!" She jigs in the middle seat. "Drive faster, Daddy!" But we were pulling into the campground loop's curve now, so we have to crawl at a snail's pace.

"We've got to retrace our steps from that day." I point at Ethan, "Minus the riding-in-the-river part of your trip, of course."

He nods, and I jet out of the truck as soon as we're at site A-68. Sadie rushes to her tent for something, but I'm already running for the Gros Ventre River like a varsity sprinter.

When I reach the spot where Ethan fell in, it's only him and me. We turn to find Sadie and Dad urging Mom on.

"I...haven't...run that far...since high school," she pants. Her eyes go wide. "Is this the place where you fell in?"

Ethan nods.

We're a good way from the edge, but it's clear how far down the river is.

"I'm so thankful you survived."

"We need to cut down this way so we can find the camp." I walk to the edge of the loose shale cliffside that Sadie and I had scrambled down after Ethan. Without the terror of his disappearing downriver, descending the cliff looks a lot more daunting this time.

"I don't think so. It's not safe!" Mom protests.

"Isaiah and I already did it. It will be fun," Sadie adds.

"Oh, Lord, help…" Mom's hand is on her heart as I ease over the edge, dropping quickly down the slick shale, half-running, half-sliding.

Ethan and Sadie outpace me, gliding down as if they're on a slip and slide.

"Wait!" Mom cries behind us.

-26-

We're already past the point of no return, and I twist at the bottom to see Mom and Dad only half-way down. Mom has a death grip on Dad's arm, and she screams like a girl the entire descent as he holds her up.

"Good job, Mom!" I hug her when they reach the bottom.

We set off along the cliff's edge as if we are searching again for a way to get Ethan out of the wind.

"Here!" Sadie cries a while later, pointing at the trail we had taken.

"A four-wheeler has been using this path. Quite

often too." Ethan's eyes are bright as he studies the hidden trail.

We round the bend to the firepit where we had started a fire to warm Ethan.

"Ugh!" Sadie makes a disgusted sound as she surveys the fresh candy wrappers strewn all over the site.

"Hang on a minute," Dad says, his voice low. "Quiet down. If a horse thief is around here, we don't know what they'll do to stay hidden."

I bite my lip. *He's right; we've got to be quiet. They could be in the woods right now watching us.*

Sadie grabs Dad's arm, scanning the treeline.

"Looks like they had a fire here last night, but it's cold now. That's a good sign. Maybe they're out," he whispers, as we gather in a tight knot.

"Honey, we've got to call the park rangers or the police," Mom says.

Dad frowns at his phone. "No cell service down here. Besides, we better have a little more evidence than four-wheeler tracks before we call."

Sadie unzips her backpack, pulling out the plaster cast. She crouches near the fresh boot print. It's an exact match! Mom and Dad glance sharply at each other.

"Stick together," Mom urges, her voice tight.

"Come on! Let's follow the trail," Ethan urges.

We set out so silently that I think, *Even Kota would be proud!*

"Here is where we turned to reach the road," Sadie whispers, pointing at the right fork in the trail.

I step confidently to the left and see bits of hay strewn here and there as far as we can see. Dad nods at me, his hand on my shoulder.

Sadie sniffs, whispering, "I smell them!"

Sure enough, the warm, earthy scent of horses reaches me. Dad makes hand signals, rearranging our group so that Mom and Sadie are at the center.

"Greg. Maybe we should just call the authorities," Mom whispers.

"There is a 99-percent chance that no one will be there. We'll be careful." Dad is now caught up in the thrill of solving the mystery too. I can tell he doesn't intend to back off now.

A few steps later, we're peering through the trees at a recently cleared area around an old, partially collapsed barn. The bright white ends of the freshly cut branches seem like signposts screaming at us. We all jump when a horse's whinny rends the air.

Sadie grips my arm hard enough to make me wince, mouthing the words, "You were right!"

"Ruth, Sadie, stay here," Dad whispers so low that I can barely catch what he says. He motions to Ethan and me, and we creep forward into the small opening.

I scan everywhere, but nothing moves. At the lopsided door of the barn, the bright glimmer of a new nail head embedded in the wood catches my eye. I pull out my nail I had picked up from the site of the stampede and hold it close to the other. *An exact match.*

This close, I see that half of the barn is collapsed,

and this end has a few new boards nailed over the openings. Something stirs inside, and Timber's nose nudges me from the dark interior.

"Hey, boy," I whisper, rubbing it.

"I think we're in the clear," Dad says in a normal tone. "Let's send half of our group to go get a cell signal near the road and call the rangers. Ethan, would you escort Aunt Ruth and Sadie to the road to make the call? I'm trusting you to keep them safe."

Ethan nods, swallowing hard at the responsibility Dad has placed on him.

-27-

Now it's only Dad and me. "Good job, son. I'm impressed how you pulled together all those loose threads together and worked out the puzzle of the missing horses."

His praise sinks deep inside where I will keep it forever.

"Isaiah, let's get under the shelter of the forest while we wait for the rangers." We crouch in the shadows, and all the forest sounds come back slowly. I hear squirrels rustling and birds flitting from branch to branch. I put my hand on Dad's arm, cocking my head and pointing to my ear.

The puttering of an ATV is growing louder.

Dad pulls me back farther into the forest. We both know there is no way the rangers could be coming already. I doubt Mom has even finished calling them yet.

Every nerve on fire, I listen as the sound comes closer. Far down the trail I catch sight of the slimmest glimmer of red.

Moments later, a four-wheeler pulls up to the barn, and a figure wearing a red flannel jacket steps off. The back of his jacket has a rip flapping in the breeze. I know exactly how his jacket was torn.

The figure turns to heave a hay bale from the back of the machine, and I manage to stifle a gasp. *I recognize the tallest teenager we met in the general store our first day here!*

Dad leans forward, whispering when the boy disappears into the barn. "Follow my lead, Isaiah; we've got to keep him here until help comes," Dad whispers. He then stomps toward the trail, making a lot of noise.

"Dad!" I hiss, my heart slamming in my chest.

"Come on, son. We've got to be near the end of this hiking trail soon," Dad booms, his voice way too loud.

The teenager rushes from the dark interior of the barn as Dad strides up. The boy's face reddens, and he crosses his arms defensively over his chest. The way his pulse is jumping in his neck makes me nervous. *What if he has a weapon?*

Dad is as cool as a cucumber while addressing the boy. "Oh, hello. It's a beautiful day for a hike."

The boy's eyes to shift side to side as he tries to decide what to say. Then I step out of the woods after Dad, making the boy flinch. Dad digs into his back pocket for a map of the park.

"Do you know how far it is to the end of the Signal Mountain Trail?"

The boy looks past me down the trail, loosening up a little, obviously thinking we're just lost hikers.

I sure hope Dad knows what he's doing.

"Signal Mountain is on the other side of the park," the boy's voice cracks on the last word.

"No!" Dad jams his finger at the flopping map, stepping up to the four-wheeler to lay the map on the square rack where the hay had been. I note the strange rectangle of bare ground under the machine, and the crisp outline of hay scattered all around.

"See, we are here—almost at the end." Dad leans over the map, his knee pressed hard against the rear tire of the ATV.

"You're way lost," the boy responds flatly, nervously shifting his weight from foot to foot. "The road is that way. You'd better head there as fast as you can so you can find your way."

But Dad's not to be put off. "Say, this is a nice machine! Is it a 500 cc?" he asks, shifting toward the handlebars as if searching for a clue to its power level.

The boy doesn't answer, which sure is rude, and I watch Dad jam his hiking boot under the rear tire. He flails for balance, stumbling with his free leg. The map wings away, floating on the breeze, and Dad's arm slams into the handlebars. The key catches the light as it's ripped from its place, hitting the rocky ground at Dad's feet. With an exaggerated stumble, his boot comes free of the tire, and he kicks the key into the undergrowth.

"No!" the boy cries, his face reddening.

"Oh, I am so sorry! Here, let's look for it." Dad is on his hands and knees now next to the boy as they paw through the pine needles. I kneel next to Dad, noticing the small, silver key ring showing just to the right in front of me. I carefully tuck it farther under cover. Dad grins at me.

"I'll never find it!" The boy's face is now a mask of anger.

Dad cocks his head, listening. Sure enough, footsteps are coming. The boy sucks in a horrified breath as Ranger Dan steps into the clearing. Boots slipping, the boy takes off into the woods. Ranger Dan is after him in a flash with an impressive tackle, and I hear the whoosh of air leave the boy's lungs in a rush.

Only a few steps behind, I hear Ethan shout, "Yes!" as he pumps his fist into the air. "I knew that kid was rotten."

-28-

The metal bleachers ping under our feet as we rush down to greet Julie. She dismounts Timber, who is sweating profusely from their barrel race.

"Did you see that, Ethan? Our fastest time yet!"

She hugs each of us in turn. "Thanks to the three of you!" Her face is radiant as she boosts Sadie into the saddle. Another rider stops next to us among the crowd, and Julie turns to her and greets her with a frosty edge to her voice. "Hey, Cindy."

"Julie, listen. I had nothing to do with what John did. He's been asking me out for a year, and I guess he thought if I won because he stole your horses, then I would go out with him. But he was wrong—dead wrong."

Julie relaxes. "Thanks, Cindy. I believe you. Well, I only need two more points to beat you. Let's promise to stay friends—no matter who wins this year."

"Deal," Cindy says with a smile as she rides off.

"Well, I've got to get on Flash for the ranch horse class. I can't thank you all enough."

After another round of hugs, Ethan's face is as red as a beet, and we head back up to Mom and Dad in the bleachers. I stuff a handful of buttery popcorn into my mouth and think about how great this trip has been.

"Mom, can I get an ice cream?" Sadie asks.

"No!" we all exclaim in unison.

-29-

Our last night in the Tetons. A shiver of sadness curls around my heart. As I stare up at the crooked tent roof, wishing the week could have lasted forever, I hear the wild howl of a wolf. Golden eyes and black fur invades my mind. *Kota.*

I ease out of my sleeping bag into the soft light of a full moon. My breath floats in the air, a dense white cloud. The full moon is so bright it's casting shadows, so I walk out to the hilltop where I can see the valley below. A herd of elk is grazing there.

I take a deep breath, absorbing the life of the Grand Tetons. Another howl rends the air, and I smile even while tears prick my eyes.

"Thank you, Kota…for everything," I whisper into the night. In the same instant, all the elk raise their heads high, bodies tense.

A gray shadow emerges from the trees, its coat lit with the moonlight, and the elk herd takes off, bounding high as they race away. The gray form chases them down the valley.

"It was you!" I say, watching as the gray wolf circles back to the valley, unable to take an elk down by itself. "You scared off John the first time he tried to steal the horses, didn't you?"

I hear a sharp bark from far to the left, and the gray wolf spins toward the sound. I suck in a breath, skin tingling. Kota is a shadow within a shadow far down the valley as he barks again, a soft welcoming sound. Turning in circles and unsure of the larger wolf, the gray wolf's ears flatten against its head before sinking to the ground.

Kota is only visible when the strong moonlight hits his coat as he works his way toward the new wolf. The encroacher rushes away when Kota gets close and then crouches down again, smiling with a funny expression, its tongue hanging out.

My heart catches in my throat. "Come on! Kota won't hurt you. Stay here, wolf."

Kota circles the smaller wolf, cautiously play-bowing and trying hard to look less scary. The gray rolls over, and Kota examines its fur. He barks again and, in a flash, they're racing down the valley. Soon, the smaller gray wolf loosens up, its back no longer hunched in fear. I know from the way Kota is dancing around like a puppy, batting gently with his front paws, that the new wolf is a female. They play in the silver light of the moon, and it seems I can see sparks of fresh life rising in the wild Teton air above them. Now Kota has a new future that no one could've imagined.

-30-

The next week, I set my math book in the back of my locker with a dull metallic thud. Max Smith is standing on the other side of my locker door; I know it long before I see him because that feeling is in my chest. I take a deep breath and shut the door. Sure enough, he's sneering down at me.

"Looks like you shrunk over summer break, Rawlings." The Arctic blast of his words hits me. But I have thick fur.

"I'm gonna make you wish you'd never set foot in this school," he threatens. He crosses his arms over his thick chest.

Inside, I see Kota, not listening to a word, facing

the long harsh winter, and surviving. I nod to myself, deciding to keep Max's words on the outside of me—just like Kota hadn't let the icy fingers of winter get inside of him. I turn and start walking down the hall, away from Max.

"Hey!" he shouts after me, "Didn't you hear me?"

I turn. "Yeah, Max, I heard you. I'm just not listening." The words come out smooth and controlled without the emotions that Max feeds on.

He frowns at me. The bell rings, and he turns, walking away.

I imagine Kota high up in the Grand Teton National Park. He's got a lot of life to live. So do I. "Thanks, boy."